CW00792588

KETO DIET MEAL PLAN AND COOKBOOK

FOR WOMEN OVER 50

Stress-Free 28-Day Meal Planning and
Delicious Low-Carb Recipes to
Lose Weight and Boost Energy.

Start a Healthy Lifestyle for a Happy Menopause

ELENORE JASLOW

Copyright © 2021 by Elenore Jaslow

All rights reserved. The content contained within this book may not be reproduced, duplicated or transmitted without direct written permission from the author or the publisher.

Under no circumstances will any blame or legal responsibility be held against the publisher, or author, for any damages, reparation, or monetary loss due to the information contained within this book. Either directly or indirectly.

Legal Notice:

This book is copyright protected. This book is only for personal use. You cannot amend, distribute, sell, use, quote or paraphrase any part, or the content within this book, without the consent of the author or publisher.

Disclaimer Notice:

Please note the information contained within this document is for educational and entertainment purposes only. All effort has been made to present accurate, up to date, and reliable, complete information. No warranties of any kind are declared or implied. Readers acknowledge that the author is not engaging in the rendering of legal, financial, medical or professional advice. The content within this book has been derived from various sources. Please consult a licensed professional before attempting any techniques outlined in this book.

By reading this document, the reader agrees that under no circumstances is the author responsible for any losses, direct or indirect, which are incurred as a result of the use of information contained within this document, including, but not limited to, – errors, omissions, or inaccuracies.

TABLE OF CONTENTS

KETO DIET MEAL PLAN FOR WOMEN OVER 50

KETO DIET COOKBOOK FOR WOMEN OVER 50

KETO DIET MEAL PLAN
FOR WOMEN OVER 50

Ketogenic Cookbook for Easy Meal Planning.

28 Days of Low-Carb Recipes to
Boost Your Metabolism and Lose Weight.

Start a Healthy Lifestyle for a Happy Menopause

INTRODUCTION

Women have likely experienced significant differences in how you must diet compared to how men can diet. They have a more challenging time losing weight because of their different hormones and how their bodies break down fats. Another factor to consider is your age group. As the body ages, it is essential to be more attentive to how you care for yourself. Aging bodies start to experience problems more quickly, which can be avoided with the proper diet and exercise plan. Keto works well for women of all ages, and this is because of how it communicates with the body. It will change the way that your body metabolizes, giving you a very personalized experience.

As we age, we naturally look for ways to hold onto our youth and energy. It's not uncommon to think about things that promote anti-aging. The great thing about the Keto diet is that it supports maximum health, from the inside out, working hard to ensure that you are in the best shape you can be.

For instance, indigestion becomes as common as you age. This happens because the body cannot break down certain foods as well as it used to. With all the additives and fillers, we all become used to putting our bodies through discomfort to digest regular meals. You will realize how your digestion will begin to change upon trying a Keto diet. You will no longer feel bloated or uncomfortable after you eat. If you notice this as a familiar feeling, you are likely not eating nutritious food enough to satisfy your needs and only result in excess calories.

Keto fills you up in all the ways you need, allowing your body to digest and metabolize all the nutrients truly. When you eat your meals, you should not feel the need to overeat to overcompensate for not having enough nutrients. Anything that takes the stress from any system in your body will become a form of anti-aging. You will quickly find this benefit once you start your Keto journey, as it is one of the first-reported changes that most participants notice. In addition to a healthier digestive system, you will also experience more regular bathroom usage, with little to none of the problems often associated with age.

While weight loss is one of the more common desires for most 50+ women who start a diet plan, the way that the weight is lost matters. If you have ever shed a lot of weight before, you have probably experienced the adverse effects of sagging or drooping skin that you were left to deal with. Keto rejuvenates the elasticity in your skin. You will be able to lose weight, and your skin will catch up. Instead of having to do copious amounts of exercise to firm up your skin, it should already be becoming firmer each day you are on the Keto diet. It is something that a lot of participants are pleasantly surprised to find out.

Women also commonly report a natural reduction in wrinkles and healthier skin and hair growth, in general. Many women who start the diet report that they notice reverse effects in their aging process. While the skin becomes healthier and suppler, it also becomes firmer. Even if you aren't presently losing weight, you will still be able to appreciate the effects that Keto brings to your skin and face. Your internal systems are becoming healthier and tend to show outside in a short amount of time. You will also begin to feel healthier. While it is possible to read about others' experiences, there is nothing like feeling this for yourself when you start Keto.

Everyone, especially women over 50, has day-to-day tasks draining and requires specific amounts of energy to complete. Aging can, unfortunately, take away from your energy reserve, even if you get enough sleep at night. It limits how you must live your life, which can become a very frustrating realization. Most diet plans bring about a stagnant feeling that you are supposed to get used to, but Keto does the exact opposite. Since your body is genuinely getting everything you need nutritionally; it will repay you with a sustained energy supply.

Another common complaint about women over 50 is that seemingly overnight, your blood sugar levels will be more sensitive than usual. While everyone must keep an eye on these levels, it is especially important for those in their 50s and beyond. High blood sugar can indicate that diabetes is on the way, but Keto can become a preventative measure. Additionally, naturally regulating elevated blood sugar levels also reduces systemic inflammation, which is also common for women over 50. You will notice that you have been feeling stiff lately, despite your efforts to exercise and stretch. This is likely due to a normal case of inflamed joints. Inflammation can also affect vital organs and is a precursor to cancer. Keto will support your path to an anti-inflammatory lifestyle.

Sugar is never great for us, but it turns out that sugar can become especially dangerous as we age. What is known as "sugar sag" can occur when you get older because the excess sugar molecules will attach themselves to the skin and protein in your body. It doesn't even necessarily happen because you are overeating sugar. Average sugar intake levels can also lead to this sagging as the sugar weakens the strength of your proteins that are supposed to hold you together. With sagging come even more wrinkles and arterial stiffening.

If you have any anti-aging concerns, the Keto diet will likely be able to address your worries. It is a diet that works extremely hard while allowing you to follow a relatively direct and straightforward guideline in return. While your motivation is necessary to form a successful relationship with Keto, you won't need to worry about doing anything "wrong" or accidentally breaking your diet. If you know how to give up your sugary foods and drinks while making sure that you consume the correct amount of carbs, you will be able to find success while on a diet.

As a woman over 50, you'll find that you will feel better, healthier, and younger, by implementing the simple steps that will tune your body into processing excess fats for energy. You'll build muscle, lose fat and look and feel younger.

THE KETO BASICS

Starting a new diet can seem overwhelming. If you are a beginner, I want to start off by telling you that you are in excellent hands. Whether you know about the ketogenic diet basics or nothing at all, you will learn everything you need to help you get started. Any time you have questions, feel free to use this book as your own personal guide. While it may seem like work at first, it will become easier with time. Soon enough, you won't need to look at the list of foods you can and cannot eat; it will just come naturally. For now, let's take a look at what exactly the ketogenic diet is and why it may work for you.

WHAT IS KETOSIS?

Ketosis may seem like a scary word, but it is a completely natural metabolic state your body will enter when there is no longer glucose for your body to run off of. Instead, your body will begin to use fat as fuel! Exciting, right? Once your body has limited access to blood sugar or glucose, your body will enter a state of ketosis. You see, as you consume a low-carb diet, the levels of insulin hormones in your body will decrease, and the fatty acids in your body will be released from the fat stores.

From this point, the fatty acids that are being released in your body are then transferred to your liver. Once in place, the fatty acids are then oxidized and turned into ketone bodies, which provide your body with energy. This process is important because the fatty acids cannot cross your blood-brain barrier, meaning it cannot provide energy to your brain (important). Once the process has occurred, ketones provide energy for your body and your brain, without ever needing glucose.

HOW TO KNOW YOU ARE IN KETOSIS

To understand whether you are in ketosis, you can take tests of urine or blood which will display a higher level of ketones in the body. But then, rather than depending on these tests, you can get a whole picture when you observe the following symptoms. They are:

Increased Thirst and Urination along with Dry Mouth

When the diet changes to a low-carbohydrate one, it can cause water retention in the body. In a diet with a high amount of carbohydrates, the extra carbs are stored as glycogen in the liver. Glycogen is bound to water molecules.

So, when you shift to a low-carb diet, the amount of glycogen stored gets diminished, which in turn means you are storing less water and therefore a higher chance of dehydration. So there is a loss of excess fluid when you move to a high-fat diet and thus can make you feel thirstier. There would be increased urination also since electrolytes are also flushed out since the ketogenic diet is naturally diuretic.

Keto Breat

Since ketone bodies called acetones escape through our breath, there is a possibility of making a person's breath smell fruity. The smell disappears in the long run. The ketone bodies can also escape through sweat.

KETOGENIC DIET FOR WOMEN

Choosing a diet that actually works for you can oftentimes seem like an impossible task. If you have tried diet after diet and you still keep failing, you are not alone! Your diet is key to your overall health. Before diving into any diet, it is vital to have all of the information. If you are a woman over fifty looking to turn your health around, the ketogenic diet may be perfect for you.

WHO CAN BENEFIT?

Before you begin any diet, you should always consult with your doctor to help start. This way, a professional will be able to help you track the changes in your body, and you will have a safe place to discuss your health and condition. In general, the ketogenic diet is beneficial for women who are:

- Not getting results from their current diet
- Binge constantly on high-carb foods
- Have issues with sex hormones
- Going through menopause

Before we go any further, it's important to know which foods are allowed and which foods are not allowed in the keto diet.

KETO APPROVED FOODS

- All natural plant and dairy fats – plant-based oils, ghee, butter, cheese and cream
- Dairy products, apart from milk (milk is not allowed because it contains high amounts of carbohydrates; however, when milk is broken down to process cheese, cream, yogurt or butter, the carbohydrates are broken down)
- Nut-based milk – coconut milk, almond milk, soy milk, hemp milk
- Low-carb vegetables – leafy greens, vegies that grow above ground, ginger, onions, garlic
- Low carb fruits – berries, kiwi
- Sugar-free chocolates and condiments
- Keto sugar substitutes

KETO NON-APPROVED FOODS

- Grains, beans, legumes, lentils, rice, oats, chickpeas, barley, wheat, corn, sorghum
- Tubers – potatoes, beets, squash, yams and other starchy veggies
- Animal milk
- High-carb fruits – apples, peaches, bananas, mangoes, pineapples, melons, etc.
- Grain flours, wheat flours, chickpea flour
- High carb processed foods.

It's important that you make a habit out of reading the nutritional labels of everything you buy for you to better control your carbohydrate intake. As a rule of thumb, always go with the natural option instead of the processed option. So, for example, instead of buying store-bought chicken broth, make your own broth at home or instead of buying processed almond milk, make your own. This way, you can control all the ingredients that go into it and avoid the preservatives used to increase the shelf life of the particular item.

HORMONES AS YOU GET OLDER

MENOPAUSE

The most common result of aging-related hormonal fluctuations is menopause. Around age 50, women's ovaries start producing decreasing quantities of progesterone and estrogen; the adrenal gland attempts to compensate by creating more follicle-stimulating hormone (FSH).

While menopause is normal and happens to most girls, a few of the signs can be bothersome or even harmful. Symptoms may include these:

- Hot flashes
- Vaginal dryness and atrophy resulting in painful intercourse
- Reduced libido
- Insomnia
- Irritability/melancholy
- Osteoporosis may increase the probability of bone fractures

Assist with Symptoms: for several decades, doctors prescribed long-term utilization of an oral estrogen/progesterone mix to relieve these symptoms.

However, a study in the early 2000s demonstrated that those taking hormone replacement therapy had a greater chance of stroke, cardiovascular disorder, breast cancer, and blood clots.

Present guidelines imply that it is fine to take progesterone and estrogen for a brief period to assist with the transition to menopause and there is ongoing research investigating the efficacy and safety of various progesterone and estrogen formulas that may possibly be utilized for longer amounts of time.

Alternative therapies, for example bioidentical hormones generated from animal or plant sources, have not yet been thoroughly assessed for safety and efficacy. So for today, try the listed below:

- Non-hormonal drugs can handle hot flashes
- Topical herbal lotion used vaginally can assist with painful sex.
- Leading a healthy lifestyle that incorporates a balanced diet, regular physical activity, and anxiety management help relieve many symptoms of menopause.

It is also important for women to have regular bone-density screenings starting at age 65 to capture osteoporosis early.

NOT-SO-TENACIOUS D

Called the sunshine vitamin, as your skin synthesizes it following exposure to the sun, vitamin D acts as a hormone to help maintain strong bones and also regulate your immune system in addition to your own muscle and nerve function. Research indicates that vitamin D might also play a part in shielding cognition: 65-or-older people, who have been deficient in vitamin D, had a 53 percent greater chance of developing dementia; due to the severely paralyzed, the risk increased by 125 percent. The capability to develop into deficient increases with age. As you get older, your skin becomes much less effective in utilizing the sun's beams to create vitamin D, which means that your body needs more.

Try this: think about a daily vitamin D supplement as you might be unable to get enough out of food and by exposure alone. While the girls in their 50s and 60s get 600 ius daily, that is probably not sufficient for everybody. In a small pilot study presented at the society for endocrinology's yearly meeting, individuals who obtained 2,000 ius per day for 2 weeks had reduced blood pressure, lower levels of the stress hormone cortisol, as well as far better fitness functionality compared to placebo takers. But do not exceed this amount. Some research has linked elevated doses to an increased chance of developing kidney stones.

CHANGE OF HEART

The prevalence of heart attack in women increases significantly as soon as they reach menopause. Estrogen helps keep blood vessels pliable, and its decrease might explain why blood pressure and LDL, or bad cholesterol, often grow in this time period. Additionally, late peri- and postmenopause are correlated with higher fat deposits around the center that has been associated with an increased risk (as much as 54 percent) of cardiovascular disease.

The fat that forms on your center is particularly poisonous: it generates compounds like inflammatory proteins called cytokines, which are associated with insulin resistance and type 2 diabetes in addition to heart disease. One possible solution would be to begin hormone treatment, but time might be crucial. Should you move on HT while you are experiencing perimenopause, it might help protect you from developing this larger belly. But should you wait till you have passed menopause, then it might be too late, if you cannot take HT or don't want to, concentrate on committing to regular exercise and eating a diet low in sugar and saturated fat and full of vegetables, fish, nuts, and lean protein.

HAVING A MEAL PLAN

When you have a complete meal plan laid out in front of you, you are in a better position to have an idea as to what your diet would look like in the days to come. If you have to spontaneously decide what you will prepare to eat every time you are in the kitchen, your chances of getting off the rails become pretty high.

You can start by first calculating how many calories you are going to consume a day.

The next step would be to decide which macronutrients will have to be incorporated and in what proportion for your body to reach that goal. Remember that the rule of thumb is 75, 20, 5: for fats, proteins, and carbs, respectively.

CALORIES AND LOSING WEIGHT

In the ketogenic diet or in any other diet regimen, you need to work your calories in order to maintain, gain, or lose weight.

Simply put, if you want to maintain weight, then you need to take in as many calories as you burn. If you want to gain weight, then you need to take in more calories than you burn. And finally, if you want to lose weight, you need to burn more calories than you take in.

Let's say that again: if you want to lose weight, then you need to burn more calories than you take in. That's the simplest formula, and it applies even in the ketogenic diet.

CALCULATING YOUR DAILY CALORIC INTAKE

Many people think that calculating your calories while you are on a keto diet is not very important, but it is always good to watch how many calories you consume a day. It would help if you calculated how many calories you get to consume every day by the idea of how much weight you want to lose.

If your body needs 2,000 calories a day, but you consume only 1,400, your body is in a caloric deficit, so it will have to tap into your body's fat reserves, and this will result in a loss of weight. There are various calculators available online that can be used to calculate your daily caloric intake taking into account your objectives, age, height, activity level, and other factors.

In general, if you want to lose weight, you need to subtract around 600 calories from your daily caloric needs.

DINING OUT

When there is so much going on in your life, it might become difficult to stick to a diet. However, you should approach the keto diet with the mindset that you are making a lifestyle change, and not that you are looking for a quick fix by following the rules of a diet. When you change your mindset and begin to incorporate the diet into various aspects of your life, you will truly begin to appreciate what you are working towards and the health benefits that you can experience by maintaining your keto lifestyle.

Being on a keto diet does not mean that you can now never eat out again or go out with your friends and enjoy yourself. You should be able to have fun, enjoy good food, and do all of the things that you love to do, otherwise your diet will feel like a prison, and you will find yourself eating cheat meals more often and going back and forth between the keto diet and not seeing any changes. Below are a few tips that you can use to eat out with the keto diet.

PLAN AHEAD

Before you head out or order in, you should take a look and see if there are any keto restaurants or restaurants that offer keto-friendly food options that are near your location. You can check this using Google or Yelp, or by typing in the keyword "keto" when searching for food on any food ordering app. Restaurants that should have keto-friendly foods are burger restaurants, Mexican restaurants, places that sell breakfast and brunch options, and places that have salad bars.

You should also make sure that you take a look at each restaurant's menu to check if there are any meals or other food items that are either marked keto or sound like they could be keto friendly. Many restaurants have updated their menus to include this type of information to help their customers who have specific dietary requirements order food. You can also call the restaurant if you are unsure about anything or if you have any questions before you place your order online or go out.

ORDERING

If you do not have much of a choice and you are ordering in or eating out at a non-keto restaurant, then you will need to select your meals carefully when you are placing your order. You should take some time and go through each item on their menu if you were not able to do so before online.

When ordering non-keto foods, you should look at the food options that have little to no carbs included in the dish, or carbs that can be removed from the dish. You should choose a meal that includes some non-starchy vegetables like arugula, asparagus, bell peppers, broccoli, brussels sprouts, cauliflower, kale, mushrooms, spinach, and tomatoes, healthy fats like avocado, and a moderate amount of protein.

When checking through their menu, you should also be aware that there are some foods that are prepared in such a way that they include added sugar and carbohydrates while they are cooking the food. Some examples of how restaurants can include added sugar and carbohydrates into a dish include coating some foods with a non-keto-friendly breading, using croutons in salads, adding syrup or jam to dishes to give them a sweet flavor, using tomato sauce or paste to give some foods an extra tangy tomato taste, thickening sauces with flour, pouring gravy over a dish, serving a dish with dried fruit, and using potatoes in some dishes, like soup and stew.

If you remove starch from a meal, such as asking them to not include a potato bake in a meal, and you are now only left with protein and nonstarchy vegetables on your plate, you should consider adding a side that is high in fat, such as avocado or egg. You could also ask them to add some butter or olive oil that can go over your vegetables, if they do not have many sides that they can offer you that are high in fats.

Another thing you should check for before you order is for condiments and other sauces. Condiments and other sauces can have many added sugars contained in them. If possible, you can ask them what they made the sauce with, or if they can remove the sauce or put it separately and not mixed in or drizzled over the food. If you order steak, you should make sure that they do not cook it with a basting like BBQ sauce and ask them to season it using only salt, pepper, and whichever other keto-friendly spice that you like that they do not mind doing for you. Otherwise, you can ask them to cook it without any spices or sauces and add your own when it arrives at your table.

There are many beverages that you should avoid on the keto diet. One can never be sure what a restaurant or takeaway puts into their drinks, so you should try to avoid drinking most of their beverage options. Beverages that you can include when ordering are infused water with cucumber, lemon, or lime, soda water, sparkling water, water, and unsweetened tea and coffee. You should ensure that they do not give you milk with your tea or coffee or ask them if they can bring you some heavy cream instead.

If you cannot find any meals on their menu to your tastes or which are not keto-friendly, then you can order a few of their sides, such as a side salad, cooked vegetables, olives, a boiled egg, scrambled egg, bacon, an omelet, and so on. If you mix a few of the different sides that they offer together, you can make your own keto-friendly meal.

If you are ever unsure about what is in a specific meal or how the restaurant prepares certain foods, then you can always ask. Most restaurant employees are happy to give you a rundown of their foods, and sometimes if they are not too busy, they can prepare a more keto-friendly version of one of their meals for you. So, do not be afraid to ask them questions.

There are some wonderful keto-friendly dessert recipes out there. However, when you go to a non-keto restaurant, you will need to look for other alternatives, especially if your group wants to stay for dessert, or you are craving something sweet when ordering from home. You should try to avoid the restaurant's dessert menu and check if they have some other options. You may need to ask someone at the restaurant if they would mix some things together for you, but you can look through the menu as well. Some dessert ideas you could order include herbal tea, a cheese platter, dark chocolate, some berries served in cream, or a coffee with cream.

When I go out, I like to order a rump or sirloin steak with a side green salad or a side of cooked vegetables, such as spinach or any other non-starchy vegetable. If you order a side salad, then you should check to make sure you can eat all the vegetables that are included in the salad, especially if you have removed a few food items from the salad. Not all salads are the same depending on the restaurant you order from, but you can generally eat a green salad without worrying if it is keto friendly. Also, if you order a cooked vegetable side, you should ask how it is prepared to make sure that they do not include any added sugars or carbohydrates in the cooking process.

JUST IN CASE

When you have been doing the keto diet for a while, you will become more familiar with the restaurants in your area and whether they have any keto-friendly options or not. If you know that you might struggle to find something at a restaurant when you are meeting up with your friends, then you might need to eat something before you leave the house and then order a side that you can nibble on while your friends are eating. That way, you will not feel left out by your friends, nor will you be hungry.

In less formal situations, such as going for a picnic or hike with friends and family, or visiting your family for a Sunday lunch, you can prepare your own meals to take with you if they are fine with you doing this (which they should not have a problem with). By doing this, you do not need to rely on anyone preparing you a separate lunch that is keto-friendly when everyone else is eating something else.

WEEK 1

MONDAY - DAY 1 - BREAKFAST
BACON & AVOCADO OMELET

PREPARATION TIME: 5 MINUTES | COOKING TIME: 5 MINUTES | SERVINGS: 1

INGREDIENTS:

1 slice crispy bacon

2 large organic eggs

5 cups freshly grated parmesan cheese

1 teaspoon finely chopped herbs

2 tablespoons ghee or coconut oil or butter

Half 1 small avocado

DIRECTIONS:

1. Prepare the bacon to your liking and set aside. Combine the eggs, parmesan cheese, and your choice of finely chopped herbs. Warm a skillet and add the butter/ghee to melt using the medium-high heat setting. When the pan is hot, whisk and add the eggs.

2. Prepare the omelet, working it towards the middle of the pan for about 30 seconds. When firm, flip and cook it for another 30 seconds. Arrange the omelet on a plate and garnish with the crunched bacon bits. Serve with sliced avocado.

NUTRITION:

Calories: 719; Fat: 63g; Protein: 30g; Carbohydrates: 3.3g.

KETO GROUND BEEF AND GREEN BEANS

PREPARATION TIME: 5 MINUTES | COOKING TIME: 10 MINUTES | SERVINGS: 2

INGREDIENTS:

1 ½ ounce butter

8 ounces green beans, fresh, rinsed and trimmed

10 ounces ground beef

¼ cup crème fraîche or home-made mayonnaise, optional

Pepper and salt to taste

DIRECTIONS:

1. Over moderate heat in a large, frying pan; heat a generous dollop of butter until completely melted.

2. Increase the heat to high and immediately brown the ground beef until almost done, for 5 minutes. Sprinkle with pepper and salt to taste.

3. Decrease the heat to medium; add more butter and continue to fry the beans in the same pan with the meat for 5 more minutes, stirring frequently.

4. Season the beans with pepper and salt as well. Serve with the leftover butter and add in the optional crème fraiche or mayonnaise, if desired.

NUTRITION:

Calories: 513; Fat: 44g; Protein: 30g; Carbohydrates: 8.5g.

MONDAY - DAY 1 - DINNER
PASTA FREE LASAGNA

PREPARATION TIME: 20 MINUTES | COOKING TIME: 56 MINUTES | SERVINGS: 12

INGREDIENTS:

2 large eggplants, cut into 1/8-inch thick slices lengthwise

Salt, as required

1 large organic egg

½ cup plus 2 tablespoons Parmesan cheese, grated and divided

15 ounces part-skim ricotta

4 cups sugar-free tomato sauce

16 ounces part-skim mozzarella cheese, shredded

2 tablespoons fresh parsley, chopped

DIRECTIONS:

1. Preheat the oven to 375°F.
2. Arrange the eggplant slices onto a smooth surface in a single layer and sprinkle with salt.
3. Set aside for about 10 minutes.
4. With a paper towel, pat dry the eggplant slices to remove the excess moisture and salt.
5. Heat a greased grill pan over medium heat and cook the eggplant slices for about 3 minutes per side.
6. Remove the eggplant slices from the grill pan and set aside.
7. In a medium bowl, place the egg, ricotta cheese and 1/2 cup of Parmesan cheese and mix well.
8. In the bottom of a 9x12-inch casserole dish, spread some tomato sauce evenly.
9. Place 5-6 eggplant slices on top of the sauce.
10. Spread some of the cheese mixture over eggplant slices and top with some of the mozzarella cheese.
11. Repeat the layers and sprinkle with the remaining Parmesan cheese.
12. Cover the casserole dish and bake for about 40 minutes.
13. Uncover the baking dish and bake for about 10 more minutes.
14. Remove the baking dish from oven and set aside for about 5-10 minutes before serving.
15. Cut into 12 equal-sized portions and serve, garnishing with fresh parsley.

NUTRITION:

Calories: 200; Fat: 1g; Protein: 18.2g; Carbohydrates: 8g.

TUESDAY - DAY 2 - BREAKFAST
MORNING COCONUT PORRIDGE

PREPARATION TIME: 1 MINUTE | COOKING TIME: 5 MINUTES | SERVINGS: 1

INGREDIENTS:

1 egg, beaten

1 tablespoon coconut milk

2 tablespoons coconut flour

2 teaspoons butter

1 cup water

1 pinch salt

2 tablespoons flax seeds

Blueberries and raspberries

DIRECTIONS:

1. Put the flax seeds, coconut flour, water, and salt into a saucepan.

2. Heat this mixture until it has thickened slightly

3. Remove the mixture from the heat. Add beaten egg and put it on the stove again. Whisk slowly until you get a creamy texture.

4. Remove from the heat, add the butter and stir.

5. Serve with coconut milk, blueberries, and raspberries.

NUTRITION:

Calories 486; Fat 27g; Protein; 15g; Carbohydrates 6g.

CHEESY TILAPIA

PREPARATION TIME: 10 MINUTES | COOKING TIME: 10 MINUTES | SERVINGS: 8

INGREDIENTS:

2 pounds tilapia fillets

½ cup Parmesan cheese, grated

3 tablespoons mayonnaise

¼ cup unsalted butter, softened

2 tablespoons fresh lemon juice

¼ teaspoon dried thyme, crushed

Salt and ground black pepper, to taste

DIRECTIONS:

1. Preheat the broiler of the oven.
2. Grease a broiler pan.
3. In a large bowl, mix together all ingredients except tilapia fillets. Set aside.
4. Place the fillets onto the prepared broiler pan in a single layer.
5. Broil the fillets for about 2-3 minutes.
6. Remove the broiler pan from the oven and top the fillets with cheese mixture evenly.
7. Broil for about 2 minutes further.
8. Serve hot.

NUTRITION:

Calories: 185; Fat: 9.8g; Protein: 23.2g; Carbohydrates: 1.4g.

TUESDAY - DAY 2 - DINNER
PAPRIKA CHICKEN

PREPARATION TIME: 10 MINUTES | COOKING TIME: 35 MINUTES | SERVINGS: 4

INGREDIENTS:

4 chicken breasts, skinless and boneless, cut into chunks

2 tablespoons paprika

2 ½ tablespoons olive oil

1 ½ teaspoons garlic, minced

2 tablespoons fresh lemon juice

Pepper

Salt

DIRECTIONS:

1. Preheat the oven to 350°F.
2. In a small bowl, mix together garlic, lemon juice, paprika, and olive oil.
3. Season chicken with pepper and salt.
4. Spread 1/3 bowl mixture on the bottom of the casserole dish.
5. Add chicken into the casserole dish and rub with dish sauce.
6. Pour remaining sauce over chicken and rub well.
7. Bake for 30-35 minutes.
8. Serve and enjoy.

NUTRITION:

Calories: 380; Fat: 22g; Protein: 14g; Carbohydrates: 2.6g.

WEDNESDAY - DAY 3 - BREAKFAST
BREAKFAST ROLL-UPS

PREPARATION TIME: 5 MINUTES | COOKING TIME: 15 MINUTES | SERVINGS: 5 ROLL-UPS

INGREDIENTS:

Non-stick cooking spray

10 slices cooked bacon

1½ cups cheddar cheese, shredded

Pepper and salt

10 large eggs

DIRECTIONS:

1. Preheat a skillet on medium to high heat, then combine two of the eggs in a mixing bowl using a whisk.

2. After the pan has become hot, lower the heat to medium-low heat, then put in the eggs. If you want to, you can use some cooking spray.

3. Season eggs with some pepper and salt.

4. Cover the eggs and leave them to cook for a couple of minutes or until the eggs are almost cooked.

5. Drizzle around 1/3 cup of cheese on top of the eggs, then place 2 strips of bacon.

6. Roll the egg carefully on top of the fillings. The roll-up will almost look like a taquito. If you have a hard time folding over the egg, use a spatula to keep the egg intact until the egg has molded into a roll-up.

7. Put aside the roll-up, then repeat the above steps until you have four more roll-ups; you should have 5 roll-ups in total.

NUTRITION:

Calories: 412.2; Fat: 31.66g; Protein: 28,21g; Carbohydrates: 2.26g.

CAULIFLOWER AND CASHEW NUT SALAD

PREPARATION TIME: 10 MINUTES | COOKING TIME: 5 MINUTES | SERVINGS: 4

INGREDIENTS:

1 head cauliflower, cut into florets

½ cup black olives, pitted and chopped

1 cup roasted bell peppers, chopped

1 red onion, sliced

½ cup cashew nuts

Chopped celery leaves, for garnish

For the dressing:

Olive oil

Mustard

Vinegar

Salt and pepper

DIRECTIONS:

1. Add the cauliflower into a pot of boiling salted water. Allow to boil for 4 to 5 minutes until fork-tender but still crisp.

2. Remove from the heat and drain on paper towels, then transfer the cauliflower to a bowl.

3. Add the olives, bell pepper, and red onion. Stir well.

4. Make the dressing: In a separate bowl, mix the olive oil, mustard, vinegar, salt, and pepper. Pour the dressing over the veggies and toss to combine.

5. Serve topped with cashew nuts and celery leaves.

NUTRITION:

Calories: 298; Fat: 20g; Protein: 8g; Carbohydrates: 4g.

WEDNESDAY - DAY 3 - DINNER
GARLICKY PRIME RIB ROAST

PREPARATION TIME: 15 MINUTES | COOKING TIME: 1 HOUR 35 MINUTES | SERVINGS: 15

INGREDIENTS:

10 garlic cloves

2 teaspoons dried thyme

2 tablespoons olive oil

Salt

Ground black pepper

1 grass-fed prime rib roast

DIRECTIONS:

1. Mix the garlic, thyme, oil, salt, and black pepper. Marinate the rib roast with garlic mixture for 1 hour.
2. Warm-up oven to 500°F.
3. Roast for 20 minutes. Lower to 325°F and roast for 65-75 minutes.
4. Remove, then cool down for 10-15 minutes, slice, and serve.

NUTRITION:

Calories: 499; Fat: 25.9g; Protein: 61.5g; Carbohydrates: 0.7g.

THURSDAY - DAY 4 - BREAKFAST
BRACING GINGER SMOOTHIE

PREPARATION TIME: 5 MINUTES | COOKING TIME: 5 MINUTES | SERVINGS: 2

INGREDIENTS:

1/3 cup coconut cream

2/3 cup water

2 tablespoons lime juice

1 ounce spinach, frozen

2 tablespoons ginger, grated

DIRECTIONS:

1. Blend all the ingredients. Add 1 tablespoon lime at first and increase the amount if necessary.

2. Top with grated ginger and enjoy your smoothie!

NUTRITION:

Calories: 82; Fat: 8g; Protein: 1g; Carbohydrates: 3g.

THURSDAY - DAY 4 - LUNCH
CHICKEN AVOCADO SALAD

PREPARATION TIME: 10 MINUTES | COOKING TIME: 10 MINUTES | SERVINGS: 3

INGREDIENTS:

2 chicken breasts, cooked and cubed

1 tablespoon fresh lime juice

2 avocados, peeled and pitted

2 Serrano chili peppers, chopped

¼ cup celery, chopped

1 onion, chopped

1 cup cilantro, chopped

1 teaspoon kosher salt

DIRECTIONS:

1. Scoop out the pulp from the avocados and place it in the bowl.
2. Mash the avocado flesh using a fork.
3. Add remaining ingredients and mix until well combined.
4. Serve and enjoy.

NUTRITION:

Calories: 236; Fat: 10.6g; Protein: 29g; Carbohydrates: 4.5g.

THURSDAY - DAY 4 - DINNER
EGG DROP SOUP

PREPARATION TIME: 5 MINUTES | COOKING TIME: 15 MINUTES | SERVINGS: 2

INGREDIENTS:

- 3 cups chicken broth
- 2 cups Swiss chard chopped
- 2 eggs, whisked
- 1 teaspoon grated ginger
- 1 teaspoon ground oregano
- 2 tablespoons coconut aminos
- Salt and pepper

DIRECTIONS:

1. Heat your broth in a saucepan.
2. Slowly drizzle in the eggs while stirring slowly.
3. Add the Swiss chard, grated ginger, oregano, and the coconut aminos. Next, season it and let it cook for 5-10 minutes.

NUTRITION:

Calories: 225; Fat: 19g; Protein: 11g; Carbohydrates: 4g.

BACON CHEESEBURGER WAFFLES

PREPARATION TIME: 10 MINUTES | COOKING TIME: 20 MINUTES | SERVINGS: 4

INGREDIENTS:

Toppings

Pepper and salt to taste

1 ½ ounces cheddar cheese

4 tablespoons sugar-free barbecue sauce

4 slices bacon

4 ounces ground beef, 70% lean meat and 30% Fat

Waffle dough

Pepper and salt to taste

3 tablespoons parmesan cheese, grated

4 tablespoons almond flour

¼ teaspoon onion powder

¼ teaspoon garlic powder

1 cup cauliflower crumbles

2 large eggs

1 ½ ounces cheddar cheese

DIRECTIONS:

1. Shred about 3 ounces of cheddar cheese, then add in cauliflower crumbles in a bowl and put in half of the cheddar cheese.
2. Put spices, almond flour, eggs, and parmesan cheese into the mixture, then mix and put aside for some time.
3. Thinly slice the bacon and cook in a skillet on medium to high heat.
4. After the bacon is partially cooked, put in the beef, cook until the mixture is well done.
5. Put the excess grease from the bacon mixture into the waffle mixture. Set aside the bacon mix.
6. Use an immersion blender to blend the waffle mix until it becomes a paste, then add half of the mix into the waffle iron and cook until it becomes crispy.
7. Repeat for the remaining waffle mixture.
8. As the waffles cook, add sugar-free barbecue sauce to the ground beef and bacon mixture in the skillet.
9. Then proceed to assemble waffles by topping them with half of the remaining cheddar cheese and half the beef mixture. Repeat this for the remaining waffles, broil for around 1-2 minutes until the cheese has melted, then serve right away.

NUTRITION:

Calories: 405; Fat: 33.9g; Protein: 18.8g; Carbohydrates: 4.4g.

FRIDAY - DAY 5 - LUNCH
SHRIMP STEW

PREPARATION TIME: 15 MINUTES | COOKING TIME: 20 MINUTES | SERVINGS: 6

INGREDIENTS:

¼ cup olive oil

¼ cup onion, chopped

¼ cup roasted red pepper, chopped

1 garlic clove, minced

1 ½ pounds raw shrimp, peeled and deveined

1 (14-ounce) can sugar-free diced tomatoes with chilies

1 cup unsweetened coconut milk

2 tablespoons Sriracha

2 tablespoons fresh lime juice

Salt and ground black pepper, to taste

¼ cup fresh cilantro, chopped

DIRECTIONS:

1. In a wok, heat the oil over medium heat and sauté the onion for about 4–5 minutes.
2. Add the red pepper and garlic and sauté for about 4–5 minutes.
3. Add the shrimp and tomatoes and cook for about 3–4 minutes.
4. Stir in the coconut milk and Sriracha and cook for about 4–5 minutes.
5. Stir in the lime juice, salt and black pepper and remove from the heat.
6. Garnish with cilantro and serve hot.

NUTRITION:

Calories: 289; Fat: 16g; Protein: 27.1g; Carbohydrates: 7g.

FRIDAY - DAY 5 - DINNER
KETO RED CURRY

PREPARATION TIME: 20 MINUTES | COOKING TIME: 15-20 MINUTES | SERVINGS: 6

INGREDIENTS:

1 cup broccoli florets

1 large handful of fresh spinach

4 tablespoons coconut oil

¼ medium onion

1 teaspoon garlic, minced

1 teaspoon fresh ginger, peeled and minced

2 teaspoons soy sauce

1 tablespoon red curry paste

½ cup coconut cream

DIRECTIONS:

1. Add half the coconut oil to a saucepan and heat over medium-high heat.

2. When the oil is hot, put the onion in the pan and sauté for 3-4 minutes, until it is semi-translucent.

3. Sauté garlic, stirring, just until fragrant, about 30 seconds.

4. Lower the heat to medium-low and add broccoli florets. Sauté, stirring, for about 1-2 minutes.

5. Now, add the red curry paste. Sauté until the paste is fragrant, then mix everything.

6. Add the spinach on top of the vegetable mixture. When the spinach begins to wilt, add the coconut cream and stir.

7. Add the rest of the coconut oil, the soy sauce, and the minced ginger. Bring to a simmer for 5-10 minutes.

8. Serve hot.

NUTRITION:

Calories: 265; Fat: 7.1g; Protein: 4.4g; Carbohydrates: 2.1g.

SATURDAY - DAY 6 - BREAKFAST
SESAME KETO BAGELS

PREPARATION TIME: 10 MINUTES | COOKING TIME: 15 MINUTES | SERVINGS: 6

INGREDIENTS:

2 cups almond flour

3 eggs

1 tablespoon baking powder

2 ½ cups Mozzarella cheese, shredded

½ cream cheese, cubed

1 pinch salt

2-3 teaspoons sesame seeds

DIRECTIONS:

1. Preheat the oven to 425°F.

2. Use a medium bowl to whisk the almond flour and baking powder. Add the mozzarella cheese and cubed cream cheese into a large bowl, mix and microwave for 90 seconds. Place 2 eggs into the almond mixture and stir in thoroughly to form a dough.

3. Part your dough into 6 portions and make into balls. Press every dough ball slightly to make a hole in the center and put your ball on the baking mat.

4. Brush the top of every bagel with the remaining egg and top with sesame seeds.

5. Bake for about 15 minutes.

NUTRITION:

Calories: 469; Fat: 39g; Protein: 23g; Carbohydrates: 9g.

SATURDAY - DAY 6 - LUNCH
HEALTHY CELERY SOUP

PREPARATION TIME: 10 MINUTES | COOKING TIME: 20 MINUTES | SERVINGS: 4

INGREDIENTS:

3 cups celery, chopped

1 cup vegetable broth

5 ounces cream cheese

1 ½ tablespoons fresh basil, chopped

¼ cup onion, chopped

1 tablespoon garlic, chopped

1 tablespoon olive oil

¼ teaspoon pepper

½ teaspoon salt

DIRECTIONS:

1. Heat some oil.
2. Add celery, onion and garlic to the saucepan and sauté for 4-5 minutes or until softened.
3. Add broth and bring to boil. Turn heat to low and simmer.
4. Add basil and cream cheese and stir until cheese is melted.
5. Season soup with pepper and salt.
6. Puree the soup until smooth.
7. Serve and enjoy.

NUTRITION:

Calories: 201; Fat: 5.4g; Protein: 5.1g; Carbohydrates: 3.9g.

SATURDAY - DAY 6 - DINNER
WINTER COMFORT STEW

PREPARATION TIME: 15 MINUTES | COOKING TIME: 50 MINUTES | SERVINGS: 6

INGREDIENTS:

2 tablespoons olive oil

1 small yellow onion, chopped

2 garlic cloves, chopped

2 pounds grass-fed beef chuck, cut into 1-inch cubes

1 (14-ounce) can sugar-free crushed tomatoes

2 teaspoons ground allspice

1 ½ teaspoons red pepper flakes

½ cup homemade beef broth

6 ounces green olives, pitted

8 ounces fresh baby spinach

2 tablespoons fresh lemon juice

Salt and freshly ground black pepper, to taste

¼ fresh cilantro, chopped

DIRECTIONS:

1. In a pan, heat the oil over high heat and sauté the onion and garlic for about 2-3 minutes.

2. Add the beef and cook for about 3-4 minutes or until browned, stirring frequently.

3. Add the tomatoes, spices and broth and bring to a boil.

4. Reduce the heat to low and simmer, covered for about 30-40 minutes or until the desired doneness of the beef.

5. Stir in the olives and spinach and simmer for about 2-3 minutes.

6. Stir in the lemon juice, salt, and black pepper and remove from the heat.

7. Serve hot with the garnishing of cilantro.

NUTRITION:

Calories: 388; Fat: 17.7g; Protein: 48.5g; Carbohydrates: 8g.

SUNDAY - DAY 7 - BREAKFAST
MATCHA GREEN JUICE

PREPARATION TIME: 10 MINUTES | COOKING TIME: 0 MINUTES | SERVINGS: 2

INGREDIENTS:

5 ounces fresh kale

2 ounces fresh arugula

¼ cup fresh parsley

4 celery stalks

1 (1-inch) piece fresh ginger, peeled

1 lemon, peeled

½ teaspoon matcha green tea

DIRECTIONS:

1. Add all ingredients into a juicer and extract the juice according to the manufacturer's method.

2. Pour into 2 glasses and serve immediately.

NUTRITION:

Calories: 113; Fat: 2.1g; Protein: 1.3g; Carbohydrates: 12.3g.

SUNDAY - DAY 7 - LUNCH
LEMONY SALMON

PREPARATION TIME: 10 MINUTES | COOKING TIME: 10 MINUTES | SERVINGS: 4

INGREDIENTS:

1 tablespoon butter, melted

1 tablespoon fresh lemon juice

1 teaspoon Worcestershire sauce

1 teaspoon lemon zest, grated finely.

4 (6-ounce) salmon fillets

Salt and ground black pepper, to taste

DIRECTIONS:

1. In a baking dish, place butter, lemon juice, Worcestershire sauce, and lemon zest, and mix well.
2. Coat the fillets with the mixture and then arrange skin side-up in the baking dish.
3. Set aside for about 15 minutes.
4. Preheat the broiler of the oven.
5. Arrange the oven rack about 6-inch from the heating element.
6. Line a broiler pan with a piece of foil.
7. Remove the salmon fillets from the baking dish and season with salt and black pepper.
8. Arrange the salmon fillets onto the prepared broiler pan, skin side down.
9. Broil for about 8-10 minutes.
10. Serve hot.

NUTRITION:

Calories: 253; Fat: 13.4g; Protein: 33.1g; Carbohydrates: 0.4g.

SUNDAY - DAY 7 - DINNER
YUMMY CHICKEN SKEWERS

PREPARATION TIME: 10 MINUTES | COOKING TIME: 10 MINUTES | SERVINGS: 8

INGREDIENTS:

2 pounds chicken breast tenderloins

1 teaspoon lemon pepper seasoning

1 teaspoon garlic, minced

1 tablespoon olive oil

1 cup of salsa

DIRECTIONS:

1. Add chicken in a zip-lock bag along with 1/4 cup salsa, lemon pepper seasoning, garlic, and oil.

2. Seal bag and shake well and place it in the refrigerator overnight.

3. Thread marinated chicken onto the soaked wooden skewers.

4. Place skewers on hot grill and cooks for 8-10 minutes.

5. Brush with remaining salsa during the last 3 minutes of grilling.

6. Serve and enjoy.

NUTRITION:

Calories: 125; Fat: 2.5g; Protein: 24g; Carbohydrates: 2.1g.

WEEK 2

MONDAY - DAY 8 - BREAKFAST
COFFEE SURPRISE

PREPARATION TIME: 5 MINUTES | COOKING TIME: 5 MINUTES | SERVINGS: 1 SERVING

INGREDIENTS:

2 heaped tablespoons flaxseed, ground

100 ml cooking cream 35% Fat

½ teaspoon cocoa powder, dark and unsweetened

1 tablespoon goji berries

Freshly brewed coffee

DIRECTIONS:

1. Mix together the flaxseeds, cream and cocoa and coffee.

2. Season with goji berries.

3. Serve!

NUTRITION:

Calories: 55; Fat: 45g; Protein: 15g; Carbohydrates: 3g.

BEEF SALAD WITH VEGETABLES

PREPARATION TIME: 10 MINUTES | COOKING TIME: 10 MINUTES | SERVINGS: 4

INGREDIENTS:

1-pound (454 g) ground beef

¼ cup pork rinds, crushed

1 egg, whisked

1 onion, grated

1 tablespoon fresh parsley, chopped

½ teaspoon dried oregano

1 garlic clove, minced

Salt and black pepper, to taste

2 tablespoons olive oil, divided

Salad:

1 cup chopped arugula

1 cucumber, sliced

1 cup cherry tomatoes, halved

1 ½ tablespoons lemon juice

Salt and pepper, to taste

DIRECTIONS:

1. Stir together the beef, pork rinds, whisked egg, onion, parsley, oregano, garlic, salt, and pepper in a large bowl until completely mixed.

2. Make the meatballs: On a lightly floured surface, using a cookie scoop to scoop out equal-sized amounts of the beef mixture and form into meatballs with your palm.

3. Heat 1 tablespoon olive oil in a large skillet over medium heat, fry the meatballs for about 4 minutes on each side until cooked through.

4. Remove from the heat and set aside on a plate to cool.

5. In a salad bowl, mix the arugula, cucumber, cherry tomatoes, 1 tablespoon olive oil, and lemon juice. Serve, season with salt and pepper.

NUTRITION:

Calories: 302; Fat: 13g; Protein: 7g; Carbohydrates: 6g.

MONDAY - DAY 8 - DINNER
CRAB-STUFFED AVOCADO

PREPARATION TIME: 20 MINUTES | COOKING TIME: 0 MINUTES | SERVINGS: 2

INGREDIENTS:

1 avocado, peeled, halved lengthwise, and pitted

½ teaspoon freshly squeezed lemon juice

4 ½ ounces Dungeness crabmeat

½ cup cream cheese

¼ cup chopped red bell pepper

¼ cup chopped, peeled English cucumber

½ scallion, chopped

1 teaspoon chopped cilantro

Pinch sea salt

Freshly ground black pepper

DIRECTIONS:

1. Brush the cut edges of the avocado with the lemon juice and set the halves aside on a plate.

2. In a bowl or container, the crabmeat, cream cheese, red pepper, cucumber, scallion, cilantro, salt, and pepper must be well-mixed.

3. Divide the crab mixture between the avocado.

4. Serve and enjoy.

NUTRITION:

Calories: 239; Fat: 11.4g; Protein: 5.9g; Carbohydrates: 3.8g.

TUESDAY - DAY 9 - BREAKFAST
COCONUT PILLOW

PREPARATION TIME: 10 MINUTES | COOKING TIME: 0 MINUTES | SERVINGS: 4 SERVINGS

INGREDIENTS:

1 can unsweetened coconut milk

Berries of choice

Dark chocolate

DIRECTIONS:

1. Refrigerate the coconut milk for 24 hours.

2. Remove it from your refrigerator and whip for 2-3 minutes.

3. Fold in the berries.

4. Season with the chocolate shavings.

5. Serve!

NUTRITION:

Calories: 50; Fat: 5g; Protein: 1g; Carbohydrates: 2g.

TUESDAY - DAY 9 - LUNCH
PARMESAN CHICKEN

PREPARATION TIME: 10 MINUTES | COOKING TIME: 35 MINUTES | SERVINGS: 4

INGREDIENTS:

1 pound chicken breasts, skinless and boneless

½ cup parmesan cheese, grated

¾ cup mayonnaise

1 teaspoon garlic powder

½ teaspoon Italian seasoning

DIRECTIONS:

1. Preheat the oven to 375°F.
2. Spray baking dish with cooking spray.
3. In a small bowl, mix together mayonnaise, garlic powder, poultry seasoning, and pepper.
4. Place chicken breasts into the prepared baking dish.
5. Spread mayonnaise mixture over chicken then sprinkles cheese on top of chicken.
6. Bake chicken for 35 minutes.
7. Serve and enjoy.

NUTRITION:

Calories: 391; Fat: 23g; Protein: 16g; Carbohydrates: 11g.

DELICIOUS TOMATO BASIL SOUP

PREPARATION TIME: 10 MINUTES | COOKING TIME: 40 MINUTES | SERVINGS: 4

INGREDIENTS:

¼ cup olive oil

½ cup heavy cream

1 pound tomatoes, fresh

4 cups chicken broth, divided

4 cloves garlic, fresh

Sea salt and pepper to taste

DIRECTIONS:

1. Preheat oven to 400°F and line a baking sheet with foil.
2. Remove the cores from your tomatoes and place them on the baking sheet along with the cloves of garlic.
3. Drizzle the tomatoes and garlic with olive oil, salt, and pepper.
4. Roast at 400°F for 30 minutes.
5. Pull the tomatoes out of the oven and place into a blender, along with the juices that have dripped onto the pan during roasting.
6. Add two cups of the chicken broth to the blender.
7. Blend until smooth, then strain the mixture into a large saucepan or a pot.
8. While the pan is on the stove, whisk the remaining two cups of broth and the cream into the soup.
9. Simmer for about ten minutes.
10. Season to taste, then serve hot!

NUTRITION:

Calories: 225; Fat: 20g; Protein: 6.5g; Carbohydrates: 5.5g

WEDNESDAY - DAY 10 - BREAKFAST
ALMOND COCONUT EGG WRAPS

PREPARATION TIME: 5 MINUTES | COOKING TIME: 5 MINUTES | SERVINGS: 4

INGREDIENTS:

5 organic eggs

1 tablespoon coconut flour

2 ½ teaspoons sea salt

2 tablespoons almond meal

DIRECTIONS:

1. Combine the ingredients in a blender and work them until creamy. Heat a skillet using the med-high temperature setting.

2. Pour two tablespoons of batter into the skillet and cook - covered for about three minutes. Turnover and cook for another 3 minutes. Serve the wraps piping hot.

NUTRITION:

Calories: 111; Fat: 8g; Protein: 8g; Carbohydrates: 3g.

WEDNESDAY - DAY 10 - LUNCH
CREAMED SPINACH

PREPARATION TIME: 10 MINUTES | COOKING TIME: 15 MINUTES | SERVINGS: 4

INGREDIENTS:

2 tablespoons unsalted butter

1 small yellow onion, chopped

1 cup cream cheese, softened

2 (10-ounce) packages frozen spinach, thawed and squeezed dry

2-3 tablespoons water

Salt and ground black pepper, as required

1 teaspoon fresh lemon juice

DIRECTIONS:

1. Melt some butter and sauté the onion for about 6–8 minutes.
2. Add the cream cheese and cook for about 2 minutes or until melted completely.
3. Stir in the water and spinach and cook for about 4–5 minutes.
4. Stir in the salt, black pepper, and lemon juice, and remove from heat.
5. Serve immediately.

NUTRITION:

Calories: 214; Fat: 9.5g; Protein: 4.2g; Carbohydrates: 2.1g.

WEDNESDAY - DAY 10 - DINNER
BEEF & MUSHROOM CHILI

PREPARATION TIME: 15 MINUTES | COOKING TIME: 3 HOURS 10 MINUTES | SERVINGS: 8

INGREDIENTS:

2 pounds grass-fed ground beef

1 yellow onion

½ cup green bell pepper

½ cup carrot

4 ounces mushrooms

2 garlic cloves

1 can sugar-free tomato paste

2 tablespoons red chili powder

1 tablespoon ground cumin

1 teaspoon ground cinnamon

1 teaspoon red pepper flakes

½ teaspoon ground allspice

Salt

Ground black pepper

4 cups water

½ cup sour cream

DIRECTIONS:

1. Cook the beef for 8-10 minutes.

2. Stir in the remaining ingredient, except for the sour cream, and boil.

3. Cook on low, covered, for 3 hours.

4. Top with sour cream and serve.

NUTRITION:

Calories: 246; Fat: 15g; Protein: 25.1g; Carbohydrates: 8.2g.

THURSDAY - DAY 11 - BREAKFAST
BAGELS WITH CHEESE

PREPARATION TIME: 10 MINUTES | COOKING TIME: 15 MINUTES | SERVINGS: 6

INGREDIENTS:

2 ½ cups Mozzarella cheese

1 teaspoon baking powder

3 ounces cream cheese

1 ½ cups almond flour

2 eggs

DIRECTIONS:

1. Shred the mozzarella and combine with the flour, baking powder, and cream cheese in a mixing container. Pop into the microwave for about one minute. Mix well.

2. Let the mixture cool and add the eggs. Break apart into six sections and shape into round bagels. Note: You can also sprinkle with a seasoning of your choice or pinch of salt if desired.

3. Bake them for approximately 12 to 15 minutes. Serve or cool and store.

NUTRITION:

Calories: 374; Fat: 31g; Protein: 19g; Carbohydrates: 8g.

PRAWNS SALAD WITH MIXED LETTUCE GREENS

PREPARATION TIME: 10 MINUTES | COOKING TIME: 10 MINUTES | SERVINGS: 4

INGREDIENTS:

½ pound (227 g) prawns, peeled and deveined

Salt and chili pepper, to taste

1 tablespoon olive oil

2 cups mixed lettuce greens

For the dressing:

Mustard

Aioli

Lemon juice

DIRECTIONS:

1. In a bowl, add the prawns, salt, and chili pepper. Toss well.

2. Warm the olive oil over medium heat. Add the seasoned prawns and fry for about 6 to 8 minutes, stirring occasionally, or until the prawns are opaque.

3. Remove from the heat and set the prawns aside on a platter.

4. Make the dressing: In a small bowl, mix the mustard, aioli, and lemon juice until creamy and smooth.

5. Make the salad: In a separate bowl, add the mixed lettuce greens. Pour the dressing over the greens and toss to combine.

6. Divide the salad among four serving plates and serve it alongside the prawns.

NUTRITION:

Calories: 228; Fat: 17g; Protein: 5g; Carbohydrates: 3g.

SPICED JALAPENO BITES WITH TOMATO

PREPARATION TIME: 10 MINUTES | COOKING TIME: 0 MINUTES | SERVINGS: 4

INGREDIENTS:

1 cup turkey ham, chopped

¼ jalapeño pepper, minced

¼ cup mayonnaise

1/3 tablespoon Dijon mustard

4 tomatoes, sliced

Salt and black pepper, to taste

1 tablespoon parsley, chopped

DIRECTIONS:

1. In a bowl, mix the turkey ham, jalapeño pepper, mayo, mustard, salt, and pepper.
2. Spread out the tomato slices on four serving plates, then top each plate with a spoonful of turkey ham mixture.
3. Serve garnished with chopped parsley.

NUTRITION:

Calories: 250; Fat: 14.1g; Protein: 18.9g; Carbohydrates: 4.1g.

FRIDAY - DAY 12 - BREAKFAST
BACON & EGG BREAKFAST MUFFINS

PREPARATION TIME: 15 MINUTES | COOKING TIME: 30 MINUTES | SERVINGS: 12

INGREDIENTS:

8 large eggs

8 slices bacon

2 green onions

DIRECTIONS:

1. Warm the oven at 350°F. Spritz the muffin tin wells using a cooking oil spray. Chop the onions and set aside.

2. Prepare a large skillet using the medium temperature setting. Fry the bacon until it's crispy and place on a layer of paper towels to drain the grease. Chop it into small pieces after it has cooled.

3. Whisk the eggs, bacon, and green onions, mixing well until all of the ingredients are incorporated. Place the egg mixture into the muffin tin (halfway full). Bake it for about 20 to 25 minutes. Cool slightly and serve.

NUTRITION:

Calories: 117; Fat: 8.6g; Protein: 8.9g; Carbohydrates: 0.6g.

MEATLESS CABBAGE ROLLS

PREPARATION TIME: 25 MINUTES | COOKING TIME: 25 MINUTES | SERVINGS: 8

INGREDIENTS:

For filling:

1 ½ cups fresh button mushrooms, chopped

3 ¼ cups zucchini, chopped

1 cup red bell pepper, seeded and chopped

1 cup green bell pepper, seeded and chopped

½ teaspoon dried thyme, crushed

½ teaspoon dried marjoram, crushed

½ teaspoon dried basil, crushed

Salt and freshly ground black pepper, to taste

½ cup homemade vegetable broth

2 teaspoon fresh lemon juice

For rolls:

8 large cabbage leaves, rinsed

8 ounces sugar-free tomato sauce

3 tablespoons fresh basil leaves, chopped

DIRECTIONS:

1. Preheat the oven to 400°F. Lightly, grease a 13x9-inch casserole dish.
2. For filling: in a large pan, add all the ingredients except the lemon juice over medium heat and bring to a boil.
3. Reduce the heat to low and simmer, covered for about 5 minutes.
4. Remove from the heat and set aside for about 5 minutes.
5. Add the lemon juice and stir to combine.
6. Meanwhile, for rolls: in a large pan of boiling water, add the cabbage leaves and boil for about 2-4 minutes.

7. Drain the cabbage leaves well.

8. Carefully, pat dry each cabbage leaf with paper towels.

9. Arrange the cabbage leaves onto a smooth surface.

10. With a knife, make a V shape cut in each leaf by cutting the thick vein.

11. Carefully, overlap the cut ends of each leaf.

12. Place the filling mixture over each leaf evenly and fold in the sides.

13. Then, roll each leaf to seal the filling and secure each with a toothpick.

14. In the bottom of the prepared casserole dish, place 1/3 cup of the tomato sauce evenly.

15. Arrange the cabbage rolls over sauce in a single layer and top with remaining sauce evenly.

16. Cover the casserole dish and bake for about 15 minutes.

17. Remove from the oven and set aside, uncovered for about 5 minutes.

18. Serve warm, garnishing with basil.

NUTRITION:

Calories: 33; Fat: 0.4g; Protein: 2.2g; Carbohydrates: 8.5g.

FRIDAY - DAY 12 - DINNER
SPINACH & CHICKEN MEATBALLS

PREPARATION TIME: 10 MINUTES | COOKING TIME: 30 MINUTES | SERVINGS: 10

INGREDIENTS:

1 ½ pounds ground chicken

8 ounces Parmigiano-Reggiano cheese, grated

1 teaspoon garlic, minced

1 tablespoon Italian seasoning mix

1 egg, whisked

8 ounces spinach, chopped

½ teaspoon mustard seeds

Sea salt and ground black pepper, to taste

½ teaspoon paprika

DIRECTIONS:

1. Mix the ingredients until everything is well incorporated.

2. Now, shape the meat mixture into meatballs. Transfer your meatballs to a baking sheet and brush them with nonstick cooking oil.

3. Bake in the preheated oven at 350°F for about 25 minutes or until golden brown. Serve with cocktail sticks and enjoy!

NUTRITION:

Calories: 207; Fat: 12.3g; Protein: 19.5g; Carbohydrates: 4.6g.

SATURDAY - DAY 13 - BREAKFAST
KALE CHIPS

PREPARATION TIME: 5 MINUTES | COOKING TIME: 12 MINUTES | SERVINGS: 2

INGREDIENTS:

1 bunch kale, removed from the stems

2 tablespoons extra virgin olive oil

1 tablespoon garlic salt

DIRECTIONS:

1. Preheat your oven to 350°F.

2. Coat the kale with olive oil.

3. Arrange on a baking sheet.

4. Bake for 12 minutes.

5. Sprinkle with garlic salt.

NUTRITION:

Calories: 100; Fat: 7g; Protein: 2.4g; Carbohydrates: 8.5g.

KETO TACO SALAD

PREPARATION TIME: 5 MINUTES | COOKING TIME: 20 MINUTES | SERVINGS: 4

INGREDIENTS:

1 pound ground beef

3 tablespoons olive oil

A dash of pepper

1 tablespoon onion powder

1 tablespoon cumin

1 tablespoon minced garlic clove

1 chopped tomato

½ cup sour cream

½ cup black olives

¼ cup cheddar cheese

2 tablespoons cilantro

1 chopped green pepper

DIRECTIONS:

1. With a taco salad, you will be able to enjoy everything that you love about tacos with a lot fewer carbohydrates! Whether you prepare this for taco Tuesday or a quick lunch, it is sure to be a crowd-pleaser!

2. Start this recipe by taking out your grilling pan and place it over a moderate temperature. As it warms up, you can add in the olive oil and let that sizzle. When you are set, add in the green pepper, spices, and ground beef. You can also use ground turkey in this recipe if that is more your style. Cook these ingredients together for ten minutes or so.

3. Next, place some mixed greens into a bowl and cover with the meat mixture you just created. If you would like some extra flavor, sprinkle some cheddar cheese over the top, along with some sour cream.

NUTRITION:

Calories: 138; Fat: 27g; Protein: 18g; Carbohydrates: 7g.

SATURDAY - DAY 13 - DINNER
ROASTED MACKEREL

PREPARATION TIME: 10 MINUTES | COOKING TIME: 20 MINUTES | SERVINGS: 2

INGREDIENTS:

2 (7-ounce) mackerel fillets

1 tablespoon butter, melted

Salt and ground black pepper, to taste

DIRECTIONS:

1. Preheat the oven to 350°F.

2. Arrange a rack in the middle of the oven.

3. Lightly, grease a baking dish.

4. Brush the fish fillets with melted butter and then season with salt and black pepper.

5. Arrange the fish fillets into the prepared baking dish in a single layer.

6. Bake for about 20 minutes.

7. Serve hot.

NUTRITION:

Calories: 571; Fat: 41.1g; Protein: 47.4g; Carbohydrates: 7g.

HERBED COCONUT FLOUR BREAD

PREPARATION TIME: 10 MINUTES | COOKING TIME: 3 MINUTES | SERVINGS: 2

INGREDIENTS:

4 tablespoons coconut flour

½ teaspoon baking powder

½ teaspoon dried thyme

2 tablespoons whipping cream

2 eggs

Seasoning:

½ teaspoon oregano

2 tablespoons avocado oil

DIRECTIONS:

1. Take a medium bowl, place all the ingredients in it and then whisk until incorporated and smooth batter comes together.

2. Distribute the mixture evenly between two mugs and then microwave for a minute and 30 seconds until cooked.

3. When done, take out bread from the mugs, cut it into slices, and then serve.

NUTRITION:

Calories: 309; Fat: 26.1g; Protein: 9.3g; Carbohydrates: 5.3g.

SUNDAY - DAY 14 - LUNCH
MEXICAN PORK STEW

PREPARATION TIME: 15 MINUTES | COOKING TIME: 2 HOURS 10 MINUTES | SERVINGS: 2

INGREDIENTS:

3 tablespoons unsalted butter

2 ½ pounds boneless pork ribs, cut into ¾-inch cubes

1 large yellow onion, chopped

4 garlic cloves, crushed

1 ½ cups homemade chicken broth

2 (10-ounce) cans sugar-free diced tomatoes

1 cup canned roasted poblano chiles

2 teaspoons dried oregano

1 teaspoon ground cumin

Salt, to taste

¼ cup fresh cilantro, chopped

2 tablespoons fresh lime juice

DIRECTIONS:

1. In a large pan, melt the butter over medium-high heat and cook the pork, onions, and garlic for about 5 minutes or until browned.

2. Add the broth and scrape up the browned bits.

3. Add the tomatoes, poblano chiles, oregano, cumin, and salt and bring to a boil.

4. Reduce the heat to medium-low and simmer, covered for about 2 hours.

5. Stir in the fresh cilantro and lime juice and remove from heat.

6. Serve hot.

NUTRITION:

Calories: 288; Fat: 10.1g; Protein: 39.6g; Carbohydrates: 8.8g.

COLD GREEN BEANS AND AVOCADO SOUP

PREPARATION TIME: 15 MINUTES | COOKING TIME: 15 MINUTES | SERVINGS: 4

INGREDIENTS:

1 tablespoon butter

2 tablespoon almond oil

1 garlic clove, minced

1 cup (227 g) green beans (fresh or frozen)

¼ avocado

1 cup heavy cream

½ cup grated cheddar cheese + extra for garnish

½ teaspoon coconut aminos

Salt to taste

DIRECTIONS:

1. Heat the butter and almond oil in a large skillet and sauté the garlic for 30 seconds.

2. Add the green beans and stir-fry for 10 minutes or until tender.

3. Add the mixture to a food processor and top with the avocado, heavy cream, cheddar cheese, coconut aminos, and salt.

4. Blend the ingredients until smooth.

5. Pour the soup into serving bowls, cover with plastic wraps and chill in the fridge for at least 2 hours.

6. Enjoy afterward with a garnish of grated white sharp cheddar cheese

NUTRITION:

Calories: 301; Fat: 3.1g; Protein: 3.1g; Carbohydrates: 2.8g.

WEEK 3

MONDAY - DAY 15 - BREAKFAST
BACON WRAPPED ASPARAGUS

PREPARATION TIME: 10 MINUTES | COOKING TIME: 20 MINUTES | SERVINGS: 6

INGREDIENTS:

1 ½ pounds asparagus spears, sliced in half

6 slices bacon

2 tablespoons olive oil

Salt and pepper to taste

DIRECTIONS:

1. Preheat your oven to 400°F.

2. Wrap a handful of asparagus with bacon.

3. Secure with a toothpick.

4. Drizzle with the olive oil.

5. Season with salt and pepper.

6. Bake in the oven for 20 minutes or until bacon is crispy.

NUTRITION:

Calories: 166; Fat: 12.8g; Protein: 9.5g; Carbohydrates: 4.7g.

CREAMY BROCCOLI AND LEEK SOUP

PREPARATION TIME: 5 MINUTES | COOKING TIME: 25 MINUTES | SERVINGS: 4

INGREDIENTS:

10 ounces broccoli

1 leek

8 ounces cream cheese

3 ounces butter

3 cups water

1 garlic clove

½ cup fresh basil

Salt and pepper

DIRECTIONS:

1. Rinse the leek and chop both parts finely. Slice the broccoli thinly.

2. Place the veggies in a pot and cover with water and then season them. Boil the water until the broccoli softens.

3. Add the florets and garlic, while lowering the heat.

4. Add in the cheese, butter, pepper, and basil. Blend until desired consistency: if too thick, use water; if you want to make it thicker, use a little bit of heavy cream.

NUTRITION:

Calories: 451; Fat: 37g; Protein: 10g; Carbohydrates: 4g.

MONDAY - DAY 15 - DINNER
GARLIC BAKED BUTTER CHICKEN

PREPARATION TIME: 10 MINUTES | COOKING TIME: 40 MINUTES | SERVINGS: 4

INGREDIENTS:

1 tablespoon rosemary leaves, fresh

3 chicken breasts, boneless, skinless (approximately 12 ounces); washed and cleaned

1 stick butter (½ cup)

½ cup Italian cheese, low Fat and shredded

6 garlic cloves, minced

Fresh ground pepper and salt to taste

DIRECTIONS:

1. Grease a large-sized baking dish lightly with a pat of butter, and preheat your oven to 375°F.

2. Season the chicken breasts with pepper and salt to taste; arrange them in the prepared baking dish, preferably in a single layer; set aside.

3. Now, over medium heat in a large skillet; heat the butter until melted, and then cook the garlic until lightly browned, for 4 to 5 minutes, stirring every now and then. Keep an eye on the garlic; don't burn it.

4. Add the rosemary; give everything a good stir; remove the skillet from heat.

5. Transfer the already prepared garlic butter over the meat.

6. Bake in the preheated oven for 30 minutes.

7. Sprinkle cheese on top and cook until the cheese is completely melted, for a couple of more minutes.

8. Remove from oven and let stand for a couple of minutes. Transfer the cooked meat to large serving plates. Serve and enjoy.

NUTRITION:

Calories: 375; Fat: 27g; Protein: 30g; Carbohydrates: 2.3g.

SHEET PAN EGGS
WITH VEGGIES AND PARMESAN

PREPARATION TIME: 5 MINUTES | COOKING TIME: 15 MINUTES | SERVINGS: 4

INGREDIENTS:

6 large eggs, whisked

Salt and pepper

1 small red pepper, diced

1 small yellow onion, chopped

½ cup diced mushrooms

½ cup diced zucchini

½ cup freshly grated parmesan cheese

DIRECTIONS:

1. Preheat the oven to 350°F and grease cooking spray on a rimmed baking sheet.

2. In a cup, whisk the eggs with salt and pepper until sparkling.

3. Add the peppers, onions, mushrooms, and courgettes until well mixed.

4. Pour the mixture into the baking sheet and scatter over a layer of evenness.

5. Sprinkle with parmesan, and bake until the egg is set for 13 to 16 minutes.

6. Let it cool down slightly, then cut to squares for serving.

NUTRITION:

Calories: 180; Fat: 10g; Protein: 14.5g; Carbohydrates: 5g.

TUESDAY - DAY 16 - LUNCH
STEAK WITH CHEESE SAUCE

PREPARATION TIME: 15 MINUTES | COOKING TIME: 17 MINUTES | SERVINGS: 4

INGREDIENTS:

18 ounces grass-fed filet mignon

Salt

Ground black pepper

2 tablespoons butter

½ cup yellow onion

5 ¼ ounces blue cheese

1 cup heavy cream

1 garlic clove

Ground nutmeg

DIRECTIONS:

1. Cook onion for 5-8 minutes. Add the blue cheese, heavy cream, garlic, nutmeg, salt, and black pepper and stir.

2. Cook for about 3-5 minutes.

3. Put salt and black pepper in filet mignon steaks. Cook the steaks for 4 minutes per side.

4. Transfer and set aside. Top with cheese sauce, then serve.

NUTRITION:

Calories: 521; Fat: 22.1g; Protein: 44.7g; Carbohydrates: 3.3g.

TUESDAY - DAY 16 - DINNER
SCRUMPTIOUS CAULIFLOWER CASSEROLE

PREPARATION TIME: 15 MINUTES | COOKING TIME: 40 MINUTES | SERVINGS: 4

INGREDIENTS:

1 large head cauliflower, cut into florets

2 tablespoons butter

2 ounces cream cheese, softened

1 ¼ cups sharp cheddar cheese, shredded and divided

1 cup heavy cream

Salt and freshly ground black pepper, to taste

¼ cup scallion, chopped and divided

DIRECTIONS:

1. Preheat the oven to 350°F.

2. In a large pan of boiling water, add the cauliflower florets and cook for about 2 minutes.

3. Drain cauliflower and keep aside.

4. For the cheese sauce: in a medium pan, add butter over medium-low heat and cook until just melted.

5. Add cream cheese, 1 cup cheddar cheese, heavy cream, salt and black pepper and cook until melted and smooth, stirring continuously.

6. Remove from heat and keep aside to cool slightly.

7. In a baking dish, place cauliflower florets, cheese sauce, and 3 tablespoons of scallion and stir to combine well.

8. Sprinkle with remaining cheddar cheese and scallion.

9. Bake for about 30 minutes.

10. Remove the casserole dish from oven and set aside for about 5-10 minutes before serving.

11. Cut into 4 equal-sized portions and serve.

NUTRITION:

Calories: 365; Fat: 33.6g; Protein: 12g; Carbohydrates: 5.6g.

CRISPY CHAI WAFFLES

PREPARATION TIME: 10 MINUTES | COOKING TIME: 20 MINUTES | SERVINGS: 4

INGREDIENTS:

4 large eggs, separated into whites and yolks

3 tablespoons coconut flour

3 tablespoons powdered erythritol

1 ¼ teaspoon baking powder

1 teaspoon vanilla extract

½ teaspoon ground cinnamon

¼ teaspoon ground ginger

Pinch ground cloves

Pinch ground cardamom

3 tablespoons coconut oil, melted

3 tablespoons unsweetened almond milk

Cocoa

DIRECTIONS:

1. Divide the eggs into two separate mixing bowls.

2. Whip the whites of the eggs until stiff peaks develop and then set aside.

3. Whisk the egg yolks into the other bowl with the coconut flour, erythritol, baking powder, cocoa, cinnamon, cardamom, and cloves.

4. Pour the melted coconut oil and the almond milk into the second bowl and whisk.

5. Fold softly in the whites of the egg until you have just combined.

6. Preheat waffle iron with cooking spray and grease.

7. Spoon into the iron for about 1/2 cup of batter.

8. Cook the waffle according to directions from the maker.

9. Move the waffle to a plate and repeat with the batter left over.

NUTRITION:

Calories: 215; Fat: 17g; Protein: 8g; Carbohydrates: 8g.

WEDNESDAY - DAY 17 - LUNCH
CREAMY KALE SALAD

PREPARATION TIME: 15 MINUTES | COOKING TIME: 0 MINUTES | SERVINGS: 3

INGREDIENTS:

1 bunch spinach

1 ½ tablespoons lemon juice

1 cup sour cream

1 cup roasted macadamia

2 tablespoons sesame seeds oil

1 ½ garlic clove, minced

½ teaspoon black pepper

¼ teaspoon salt

2 tablespoons lime juice

1 bunch kale

Toppings

1 ½ avocado, diced

¼ cup pecans, chopped

DIRECTIONS:

1. Confirm that you have all the ingredients. Chop the kale, wash it, then remove the ribs.

2. Now transfer kale to a large bowl.

3. Add sour cream, lime juice, macadamia, sesame seeds oil, pepper, salt, garlic.

4. Finally, mix thoroughly. Top with your avocado and pecans. Serve and enjoy.

NUTRITION:

Calories: 291; Fat: 5.1g; Protein: 11.8g; Carbohydrates: 4.3g.

WEDNESDAY - DAY 17 - DINNER
SHRIMP CASSEROLE

PREPARATION TIME: 15 MINUTES | COOKING TIME: 30 MINUTES | SERVINGS: 6

INGREDIENTS:

¼ cup unsalted butter

1 tablespoon garlic, minced

1 ½ pounds large shrimp, peeled and deveined

¾ teaspoon dried oregano, crushed

¼ teaspoon red pepper flakes, crushed

¼ cup fresh parsley, chopped

½ cup homemade chicken broth

1 tablespoon fresh lemon juice

1 (14½-ounce) can sugar-free diced tomatoes, drained

4 ounces feta cheese, crumbled

DIRECTIONS:

1. Preheat the oven to 350°F.

2. In a large wok, melt butter over medium-high heat and sauté the garlic for about 1 minute.

3. Add the shrimp, oregano and red pepper flakes and cook for about 4–5 minutes.

4. Stir in the parsley and salt and immediately transfer into a casserole dish evenly.

5. In the same wok, add broth and lemon juice over medium heat and simmer for about 2–3 minutes or until liquid reduces to half.

6. Stir in tomatoes and cook for about 2–3 minutes.

7. Pour the tomato mixture over shrimp mixture evenly and sprinkle with cheese.

8. Bake for approximately 15–20 minutes or until top becomes golden-brown.

9. Remove from the oven and serve hot.

NUTRITION:

Calories: 272; Fat: 13.9g; Protein: 29.8g; Carbohydrates: 6g.

THURSDAY - DAY 18 - BREAKFAST
LEMON & CUCUMBER JUICE

PREPARATION TIME: 10 MINUTES | COOKING TIME: 0 MINUTES | SERVINGS: 2

INGREDIENTS:

2 large cucumbers, sliced

2 apples, cored and sliced

4 celery stalks

1 (1-inch) piece fresh ginger, peeled

1 lemon, peeled

DIRECTIONS:

1. Add all ingredients into a juicer and extract the juice according to the manufacturer's method.

2. Pour into 2 glasses and serve immediately.

NUTRITION:

Calories: 230; Fat: 2.1g; Protein: 1.2g; Carbohydrates: 1.3g.

THURSDAY - DAY 18 - LUNCH
VEGETABLE PATTIES

PREPARATION TIME: 15 MINUTES | COOKING TIME: 35 MINUTES | SERVINGS: 4

INGREDIENTS:

1 tablespoon olive oil

1 onion, chopped

1 garlic clove, minced

1/2 head cauliflower, grated

1 carrot, shredded

3 tablespoons coconut flour

1/2 cup Gruyere cheese, shredded

1/2 cup Parmesan cheese, grated

2 eggs, beaten

1/2 teaspoon dried rosemary

Salt and black pepper, to taste

DIRECTIONS:

1. Cook onion and garlic in warm olive oil over medium heat, until soft, for about 3 minutes.

2. Stir in grated cauliflower and carrot and cook for a minute; allow cooling and set aside.

3. To the cooled vegetables, add the rest of the ingredients, form balls from the mixture, then press each ball to form a burger patty.

4. Set oven to 400°F and bake the burgers for 20 minutes.

5. Flip and bake for another 10 minutes or until the top becomes golden brown.

NUTRITION:

Calories: 315; Fat: 12.1g; Protein: 5.8g; Carbohydrates: 3.3g.

THURSDAY - DAY 18 - DINNER
CHICKEN ENCHILADA SOUP

PREPARATION TIME: 10 MINUTES | COOKING TIME: 45 MINUTES | SERVINGS: 4

INGREDIENTS:

½ cup fresh cilantro, chopped

1 ¼ teaspoons chili powder

1 cup fresh tomatoes, diced

1 medium yellow onion, diced

1 small red bell pepper, diced

1 tablespoon cumin, ground

1 tablespoon extra-virgin olive oil

1 tablespoon lime juice, fresh

1 teaspoon dried oregano

2 cloves garlic, minced

2 large stalks celery, diced

4 cups chicken broth

8 ounces chicken thighs, boneless & skinless, shredded

8 ounces cream cheese, softened

DIRECTIONS:

1. In a pot over medium heat, warm olive oil.

2. Once hot, add celery, red pepper, onion, and garlic. Cook for about 3 minutes or until shiny.

3. Stir the tomatoes into the pot and let cook for another 2 minutes.

4. Add seasonings to the pot, stir in chicken broth and bring to a boil.

5. Once boiling, drop the heat to low and allow to simmer for 20 minutes.

6. Once simmered, add the cream cheese and allow the soup to return to a boil.

7. Drop the heat once again and let it simmer for another 20 minutes.

8. Stir the shredded chicken into the soup, along with the lime juice and the cilantro.

9. Spoon into bowls and serve hot!

NUTRITION:

Calories: 420; Fat: 29.5g; Protein: 27g; Carbohydrates: 12g.

CLASSIC WESTERN OMELET

PREPARATION TIME: 5 MINUTES | COOKING TIME: 10 MINUTES | SERVINGS: 1

INGREDIENTS:

2 teaspoons coconut oil

3 large eggs, whisked

1 tablespoon heavy cream

Salt and pepper

¼ cup diced green pepper

¼ cup diced yellow onion

¼ cup diced ham

DIRECTIONS:

1. In a small bowl, whisk the eggs, heavy cream, salt, and pepper.

2. Heat up 1 teaspoon of coconut oil over medium heat in a small skillet.

3. Add the peppers and onions, then sauté the ham for 3 to 4 minutes.

4. Spoon the mixture in a cup, and heat the skillet with the remaining oil.

5. Pour in the whisked eggs and cook until the egg's bottom begins to set.

6. Tilt the pan and cook until almost set to spread the egg.

7. Spoon the ham and veggie mixture over half of the omelet and turn over.

8. Let cook the omelet until the eggs are set and then serve hot.

NUTRITION:

Calories: 415; Fat: 32.5g; Protein: 2.5g; Carbohydrates: 6.5g.

FRIDAY - DAY 19 - LUNCH
HERBED SALMON

PREPARATION TIME: 10 MINUTES | COOKING TIME: 8 MINUTES | SERVINGS: 4

INGREDIENTS:

2 garlic cloves, minced

1 teaspoon dried oregano, crushed

1 teaspoon dried basil, crushed

Salt and ground black pepper, to taste

¼ cup olive oil

2 tablespoons fresh lemon juice

4 (4-ounce) salmon fillets

DIRECTIONS:

1. For salmon: In a large bowl, add all ingredients (except salmon) and mix well.
2. Add salmon and coat with marinade generously.
3. Cover and refrigerate to marinate for at least 1 hour.
4. Preheat the grill to medium-high heat. Grease the grill grate.
5. Place the salmon onto the grill and cook for about 4 minutes per side.
6. Serve hot.

NUTRITION:

Calories: 263; Fat: 19.7g; Protein: 22.2g; Carbohydrates: 0.9g.

SPINACH AND ZUCCHINI LASAGNA

PREPARATION TIME: 15 MINUTES | COOKING TIME: 45 MINUTES | SERVINGS: 4

INGREDIENTS:

2 zucchinis, sliced

Salt and black pepper to taste

2 cups ricotta cheese

2 cups shredded mozzarella cheese

3 cups tomato sauce

1 cup baby spinach

DIRECTIONS:

1. Let the oven heat to 375° and grease a baking dish with cooking spray.

2. Put the zucchini slices in a colander and sprinkle with salt.

3. Let sit and drain liquid for 5 minutes and pat dry with paper towels.

4. Mix the ricotta, mozzarella cheese, salt, and black pepper to evenly combine and spread 1/4 cup of the mixture in the bottom of the baking dish.

5. Layer 1/3 of the zucchini slices on top spread 1 cup of tomato sauce over, and scatter a 1/3 cup of spinach on top. Repeat process.

6. Grease one end of foil with cooking spray and cover the baking dish with the foil.

7. Let it bake for about 35 minutes. And bake further for 5 to 10 minutes or until the cheese has a nice golden-brown color.

8. Remove the dish, sit for 5 minutes, make slices of the lasagna, and serve warm.

NUTRITION:

Calories: 376; Fat: 14.1g; Protein: 9.5g; Carbohydrates: 2.1g.

SATURDAY - DAY 20 - BREAKFAST
FIVE GREENS SMOOTHIE

PREPARATION TIME: 10 MINUTES | COOKING TIME: 0 MINUTES | SERVINGS: 3

INGREDIENTS:

6 kale leaves, chopped

3 celery stalks, chopped

1 ripe avocado, skinned, pitted, sliced

1 cup of ice cubes

2 cups spinach, chopped

1 large cucumber, peeled and chopped

Chia seeds to garnish

DIRECTIONS:

1. In a blender, add the kale, celery, avocado, and ice cubes, and blend for 45 seconds. Add the spinach and cucumber, and process for another 45 seconds until smooth.

2. Pour the smoothie into glasses, garnish with chia seeds, and serve the drink immediately.

NUTRITION:

Calories: 124; Fat: 7.8g; Protein: 3.2g; Carbohydrates: 3.5g.

SATURDAY - DAY 20 - LUNCH
OMELET-STUFFED PEPPERS

PREPARATION TIME: 5 MINUTES | COOKING TIME: 20 MINUTES | SERVINGS: 2

INGREDIENTS

1 large green bell pepper, halved, cored

2 eggs

2 slices of bacon, chopped, cooked

2 tablespoons grated parmesan cheese

Seasoning:

1/3 teaspoon salt

¼ teaspoon ground black pepper

DIRECTIONS:

1. Turn on the oven, then set it to 400°F, and let preheat.

2. Then take a baking dish, pour in 1 tbsp. water, place bell pepper halved in it, cut-side up, and bake for 5 minutes.

3. Meanwhile, crack eggs in a bowl, add chopped bacon and cheese, season with salt and black pepper, and whisk until combined.

4. After 5 minutes of baking time, remove the baking dish from the oven, evenly fill the peppers with egg mixture and continue baking for 15 to 20 minutes until eggs have set.

5. Serve.

NUTRITION:

Calories: 428; Fat: 35.2g; Protein: 23.5g; Carbohydrates: 4.3g.

SATURDAY - DAY 20 - DINNER
WEEKEND DINNER STEW

PREPARATION TIME: 15 MINUTES | COOKING TIME: 55 MINUTES | SERVINGS: 6

INGREDIENTS:

1 ½ pounds grass-fed beef stew meat, trimmed and cubed into 1-inch size

Salt and freshly ground black pepper, to taste

1 tablespoon olive oil

1 cup homemade tomato puree

4 cups homemade beef broth

2 cups zucchini, chopped

2 celery ribs, sliced

½ cup carrots, peeled and sliced

2 garlic cloves, minced

½ tablespoon dried thyme

1 teaspoon dried parsley

1 teaspoon dried rosemary

1 tablespoon paprika

1 teaspoon onion powder

1 teaspoon garlic powder

DIRECTIONS:

1. In a large bowl, add the beef cubes, salt, and black pepper and toss to coat well.
2. In a large pan, heat the oil over medium-high heat and cook the beef cubes for about 4-5 minutes or until browned.
3. Add the remaining ingredients and stir to combine.
4. Increase the heat to high and bring to a boil.
5. Reduce the heat to low and simmer, covered for about 40-50 minutes.
6. Stir in the salt and black pepper and remove from the heat.
7. Serve hot.

NUTRITION:

Calories: 293; Fat: 10.7g; Protein: 9.3g; Carbohydrates: 8g.

BACON & CHEESE FRITTATA

PREPARATION TIME: 5 MINUTES | COOKING TIME: 35 MINUTES | SERVINGS: 6

INGREDIENTS:

- 1 cup heavy cream
- 6 eggs
- 5 crispy slices of bacon
- 2 chopped green onions
- 4 ounces cheddar cheese

DIRECTIONS:

1. Warm the oven temperature to reach 350°F.

2. Whisk the eggs and seasonings. Empty into the pie pan and top off with the remainder of the ingredients. Bake for 30-35 minutes. Wait for a few minutes before serving for best results.

NUTRITION:

Calories: 320; Fat: 29g; Protein: 13g; Carbohydrates: 2g.

SUNDAY - DAY 21 - LUNCH
LEMON ROSEMARY CHICKEN THIGHS

PREPARATION TIME: 10 MINUTES | COOKING TIME: 45 MINUTES | SERVINGS: 4

INGREDIENTS:

4 chicken thighs, skinless

2 garlic cloves, roughly chopped

4 sprigs of Rosemary, fresh

1 lemon, medium

2 tablespoons butter

Pepper, and salt to taste

DIRECTIONS:

1. Preheat your oven to 400°F in advance and heat up a cast-iron skillet over high heat as well.

2. Season both sides of the meat with pepper, and salt. When the skillet is hot; carefully place the coated thighs, preferably skin side down into the hot skillet, and sear them for 4 to 5 minutes, until nicely brown.

3. Carefully flip and flavor the thighs with the lemon juice (only use ½ of the lemon). Quarter the leftover lemon halves and throw the pieces into the pan with the chicken.

4. Add the chopped garlic cloves together with some rosemary into the skillet.

5. Place the skillet inside the oven and bake for 30 minutes.

6. Remove the skillet from the oven. To add flavor, moisture, and more crispiness; add a portion of butter over the chicken thighs. Bake for 10 more minutes.

7. Serve hot and enjoy.

NUTRITION:

Calories: 159; Fat: 8.8g; Protein: 13.9g; Carbohydrates: 6.9g.

NEW ENGLAND SALMON PIE

PREPARATION TIME: 20 MINUTES | COOKING TIME: 50 MINUTES | SERVINGS: 5

INGREDIENTS:

For crust:

¾ cup almond flour

4 tablespoons coconut flour

4 tablespoons sesame seeds

1 tablespoon psyllium husk powder

1 teaspoon organic baking powder

Pinch of salt

1 organic egg

3 tablespoons olive oil

4 tablespoons water

For filling:

8 ounces salmon fillets

4 ¼ ounces cream cheese, softened

1 ¼ cups cheddar cheese, shredded

1 cup mayonnaise

3 organic eggs

2 tablespoons fresh dill, finely chopped

½ teaspoon onion powder

¼ teaspoon ground black pepper

DIRECTIONS:

1. Preheat the oven to 350°F. Line a 10-inch springform pan with parchment paper.

2. For crust: place all the ingredients in a food processor, fitted with a plastic pastry blade and pulse until a dough ball is formed.

3. Place the dough into prepared springform pan and with your fingers, gently press in the bottom.

4. Bake for about 12-15 minutes or until lightly browned.

5. Remove the pie crust from the oven and let it cool slightly.

6. Meanwhile, for filling: in a bowl add all the ingredients and mix well.

7. Place the cheese mixture over the pie crust evenly.

8. Bake for about 35 minutes or until the pie is golden brown.

9. Remove the pie from oven and let it cool slightly.

10. Cut into 5 equal-sized slices and serve warm.

NUTRITION:

Calories: 762; Fat: 70g; Protein: 24.8g; Carbohydrates: 10.8g.

WEEK 4

MONDAY - DAY 22 - BREAKFAST
ITALIAN-STYLE ASPARAGUS WITH CHEESE

PREPARATION TIME: 10 MINUTES | COOKING TIME: 10 MINUTES | SERVINGS: 2

INGREDIENTS:

½ pound asparagus spears, trimmed, cut into bite-sized pieces

1 teaspoon Italian spice blend

½ tablespoon lemon juice

1 tablespoon extra-virgin olive oil

4 tablespoons Romano cheese, freshly grated

DIRECTIONS:

1. Bring a saucepan of lightly salted water to a boil. Turn the heat to medium-low. Add the asparagus spears and cook for approximately 3 minutes. Drain and transfer to a serving bowl.

2. Add the Italian spice blend, lemon juice, and extra-virgin olive oil; toss until well coated.

3. Top with Romano cheese and serve immediately. Bon appétit!

NUTRITION:

Calories: 193; Fat: 14.1g; Protein: 11.5g; Carbohydrates: 5.6g.

FRESH SUMMER SALAD

PREPARATION TIME: 3 MINUTES | COOKING TIME: 0 MINUTES | SERVINGS: 4

INGREDIENTS:

2 tablespoons olive oil

1 tablespoon thyme

1 tablespoon oregano

¼ cup ricotta cheese

1 leaf, chopped basil

1 tablespoon balsamic vinegar

1 sliced cucumber

3 sliced tomatoes

5 sliced radishes

1 sliced onion

DIRECTIONS:

Don't be fooled by the name; this salad can be enjoyed at any time of the year! If you are look-ing for a meatless dish, this is the perfect recipe for you!

1. The first step for this recipe is to make your ricotta cheese. You can complete this in a small bowl by mixing the thyme, oregano, basil with the ricotta cheese.

2. Next, make your own dressing! For this task, whisk your vinegar and olive oil together. Once this is complete, season however you like.

3. Finally, take some time to slice and dice the vegetables according to the directions above. When your veggies are all set, assemble them in your serving dishes and pour the dressing generously over the top. As a final touch, dollop your ricotta cheese over your salad, and then your salad will be ready for serving.

NUTRITION:

Calories: 158; Fat: 19g; Protein: 16g; Carbohydrates: 4g.

MONDAY - DAY 22 - DINNER
MEATBALLS CURRY

PREPARATION TIME: 15 MINUTES | COOKING TIME: 25 MINUTES | SERVINGS: 6

INGREDIENTS:

For meatballs:

1 pound lean ground pork

2 organic eggs

3 tablespoons yellow onion

¼ cup fresh parsley leaves

¼ teaspoon fresh ginger

2 garlic cloves

1 jalapeño pepper

1 teaspoon Erythritol

1 tablespoon red curry paste

3 tablespoons olive oil

For curry:

1 yellow onion

Salt

2 garlic cloves

¼ teaspoon ginger

2 tablespoons red curry paste

1 can unsweetened coconut milk

Ground black pepper

¼ cup fresh parsley

DIRECTIONS:

For meatballs:

1. Mix all the ingredients for the meatballs, except oil. Make small-sized balls from the mixture.

2. Cook meatballs for 3-5 minutes. Transfer and put aside.

For curry:

3. Sauté onion and salt for 4-5 minutes. Add the garlic and ginger. Add the curry paste and sauté for 1-2 minutes. Add coconut milk, and meatballs, then simmer.

4. Simmer again for 10-12 minutes. Put salt and black pepper. Remove, then serve with fresh parsley.

NUTRITION:

Calories. 444; Fat: g; Protein: 17g; Carbohydrates: 8.6g

BLT PARTY BITES

PREPARATION TIME: 35 MINUTES | COOKING TIME: 0 MINUTE | SERVINGS: 8

INGREDIENTS:

4 ounces bacon, chopped

3 tablespoons panko breadcrumbs

1 tablespoon Parmesan cheese, grated

1 teaspoon mayonnaise

1 teaspoon lemon juice

Salt to taste

½ heart Romaine lettuce, shredded

6 cocktail tomatoes

DIRECTIONS:

1. Put the bacon in a pan over medium heat.
2. Fry until crispy.
3. Transfer bacon to a plate lined with paper towel.
4. Add breadcrumbs and cook until crunchy.
5. Transfer breadcrumbs to another plate also lined with paper towel.
6. Sprinkle Parmesan cheese on top of the breadcrumbs.
7. Mix the mayonnaise, salt and lemon juice.
8. Toss the Romaine in the mayo mixture.
9. Slice each tomato on the bottom to create a flat surface so it can stand by itself.
10. Slice the top off as well.
11. Scoop out the insides of the tomatoes.
12. Stuff each tomato with the bacon, Parmesan, breadcrumbs and top with the lettuce.

NUTRITION:

Calories: 107; Fat: 6.5g; Protein: 6.5g; Carbohydrates: 5.4g.

GRILLED HALLOUMI CHEESE WITH EGGS

PREPARATION TIME: 15 MINUTES | COOKING TIME: 15 MINUTES | SERVINGS: 4

INGREDIENTS:

4 slices Halloumi cheese

3 teaspoons olive oil

1 teaspoon dried Greek seasoning blend

1 tablespoon olive oil

6 eggs, beaten

½ teaspoon sea salt

¼ teaspoon crushed red pepper flakes

1 ½ cups avocado, pitted and sliced

1 cup grape tomatoes, halved

4 tablespoons pecans, chopped

DIRECTIONS:

1. Preheat your grill to medium.
2. Set the Halloumi in the center of a piece of heavy-duty foil.
3. Sprinkle oil over the Halloumi and apply the Greek seasoning blend.
4. Close the foil to create a packet.
5. Grill for about 15 minutes, then slice into four pieces.
6. In a frying pan, warm one tablespoon of oil and cook the eggs.
7. Stir well to create large and soft curds—season with salt and pepper.
8. Put the eggs and grilled cheese on a serving bowl.
9. Serve alongside tomatoes and avocado, decorated with chopped pecans.

NUTRITION:

Calories: 219; Fat: 5.1g; Protein: 3.9g; Carbohydrates: 1.5g.

YELLOW CHICKEN SOUP

PREPARATION TIME: 15 MINUTES | COOKING TIME: 25 MINUTES | SERVINGS: 5

INGREDIENTS:

2 ½ teaspoons ground turmeric

1 ½ teaspoons ground cumin

1/8 teaspoon cayenne pepper

2 tablespoons butter, divided

1 small yellow onion, chopped

2 cups cauliflower, chopped

2 cups broccoli, chopped

4 cups homemade chicken broth

1 ½ cups water

1 teaspoon fresh ginger root, grated

1 bay leaf

2 cups Swiss chard, stemmed and chopped finely

½ cup unsweetened coconut milk

3 (4-ounce) grass-fed boneless, skinless chicken thighs, cut into bite-size pieces

2 tablespoons fresh lime juice

DIRECTIONS:

1. In a small bowl, mix together the turmeric, cumin, and cayenne pepper and set aside.

2. In a large pan, melt 1 tablespoon of butter over medium heat and sauté the onion for about 3-4 minutes.

3. Add the cauliflower, broccoli, and half of the spice mixture and cook for another 3-4 minutes.

4. Add the broth, water, ginger, and bay leaf and bring to a boil.

5. Reduce the heat to low and simmer for about 8-10 minutes.

6. Stir in the Swiss chard and coconut milk and cook for about 1-2 minutes.

7. Meanwhile, in a large skillet, melt the remaining butter over medium heat and sear the chicken pieces for about 5 minutes.

8. Stir in the remaining spice mix and cook for about 5 minutes, stirring frequently.

9. Transfer the soup into serving bowls and top with the chicken pieces.

10. Drizzle with lime juice and serve.

NUTRITION:

Calories: 258; Fat: 16.8g; Protein: 18.4g; Carbohydrates: 8.4g.

WEDNESDAY - DAY 24 - BREAKFAST
ALMOND BUTTER MUFFINS

PREPARATION TIME: 10 MINUTES | COOKING TIME: 25 MINUTES | SERVINGS: 6

INGREDIENTS:

1 cups almond flour

½ cup powdered erythritol

1 teaspoons baking powder

¼ teaspoon salt

¾ cup almond butter, warmed

¾ cup unsweetened almond milk

2 large eggs

DIRECTIONS:

1. Preheat the oven to 350°F, and line a paper liner muffin pan.

2. In a mixing bowl, whisk the almond flour and the erythritol, baking powder, and salt.

3. Whisk the almond milk, almond butter, and the eggs together in a separate bowl.

4. Drop the wet ingredients into the dry until just mixed together.

5. Spoon the batter into the prepared pan and bake for 22 to 25 minutes until clean comes out the knife inserted in the middle.

6. Let cool and enjoy.

NUTRITION:

Calories: 135; Fat: 11g; Protein: 6g; Carbohydrates: 4g.

WEDNESDAY - DAY 24 - LUNCH
GRILLED STEAK

PREPARATION TIME: 15 MINUTES | COOKING TIME: 12 MINUTES | SERVINGS: 6

INGREDIENTS:

1 teaspoon lemon zest

1 garlic clove

1 tablespoon red chili powder

1 tablespoon paprika

1 tablespoon ground coffee

Salt

Ground black pepper

2 grass-fed skirt steaks

DIRECTIONS:

1. Mix all the ingredients except steaks. Marinate the steaks and keep aside for 30-40 minutes.

2. Grill the steaks for 5-6 minutes per side. Remove, then cool before slicing. Serve.

NUTRITION:

Calories: 473; Fat: 17.6g; Protein: 60.8g; Carbohydrates: 1.6g.

WEDNESDAY - DAY 24 - DINNER
TURKISH STYLE BELL PEPPERS

PREPARATION TIME: 15 MINUTES | COOKING TIME: 50 MINUTES | SERVINGS: 4

INGREDIENTS:

4 large organic eggs

½ cup plus 2 tablespoons Parmesan cheese, grated and divided

½ cup mozzarella cheese, shredded

½ cup ricotta cheese

1 teaspoon garlic powder

¼ teaspoon dried parsley

2 medium bell peppers, cut in half and seeded

¼ cup fresh baby spinach leaves

DIRECTIONS:

1. Preheat the oven to 375°F and lightly, grease a baking dish.

2. In a small food processor, place the eggs, ½ cup of Parmesan, mozzarella, ricotta cheese, garlic powder and parsley and pulse until well combined.

3. Arrange the bell pepper halves into prepared baking dish, cut side up.

4. Place the cheese mixture into each pepper half and top each with a few spinach leaves.

5. With a fork, push the spinach leaves into the cheese mixture.

6. With a piece of foil, cover the baking dish and bake for about 35-45 minutes.

7. Now, set the oven to broiler on high.

8. Top each bell pepper half with the remaining Parmesan cheese and broil for about 3-5 minutes.

9. Remove from the oven and serve hot.

NUTRITION:

Calories: 191; Fat: 11.2g; Protein: 16.6g; Carbohydrates: 7g.

THURSDAY - DAY 25 - BREAKFAST
BERRY SOY YOGURT PARFAIT

PREPARATION TIME: 2-4 MINUTES | COOKING TIME: 0 MINUTES | SERVINGS: 1

INGREDIENTS:

One carton vanilla cultured soy yogurt

¼ cup granola (gluten-free)

1 cup berries (you can take strawberries, blueberries, raspberries, blackberries)

DIRECTIONS:

1. Put half of the yogurt in a glass jar or serving dish.

2. On the top put half of the berries.

3. Then sprinkle with half of granola

4. Repeat layers.

NUTRITION:

Calories: 244; Fat: 3.1g; Protein: 1.4g; Carbohydrates: 11.3g.

SESAME CHICKEN SALAD

PREPARATION TIME: 20 MINUTES | COOKING TIME: 0 MINUTES | SERVINGS: 4

INGREDIENTS:

1 tablespoon sesame seeds

1 cucumber, peeled, halved lengthwise, and sliced

3.5 ounces cabbage, chopped

2 ounces pak choi, finely chopped

½ red onion, thinly sliced

0.7-ounce large parsley, chopped

5 ounces cooked chicken, minced

For the dressing:

1 tablespoon extra virgin olive oil

1 teaspoon sesame oil

1 lime juice

1 teaspoon light honey

2 teaspoons soy sauce

DIRECTIONS:

1. Roast your sesame seeds in a dry pan for 2 minutes until they become slightly golden and fragrant.

2. Transfer to a plate to cool.

3. In a small bowl, mix olive oil, sesame oil, lime juice, honey, and soy sauce to prepare the dressing.

4. Place the cucumber, black cabbage, pak-choi, red onion, and parsley in a large bowl and mix gently.

5. Pour over the dressing and mix again.

6. Distribute the salad between two dishes and complete with the shredded chicken. Sprinkle with sesame seeds just before serving.

NUTRITION:

Calories: 345; Fat: 5g; Protein: 4g; Carbohydrates: 10g.

THURSDAY - DAY 25 - DINNER
BUTTERED SALMON

PREPARATION TIME: 10 MINUTES | COOKING TIME: 10 MINUTES | SERVINGS: 4

INGREDIENTS:

4 (5-ounce) skin-on, boneless salmon fillets

Salt and ground black pepper, to taste

1 tablespoon olive oil

3 tablespoons butter

2 tablespoons lemon juice

2 tablespoons fresh rosemary, minced

1 teaspoon lemon zest, grated

DIRECTIONS:

1. Season the salmon fillets with salt and black pepper evenly.

2. In a non-stick wok, heat oil over medium heat.

3. Place the salmon fillets, skin side down, and cook for about 3-5 minutes, without stirring.

4. Flip the salmon fillets and cook for about 2 minutes.

5. Add the butter, lemon juice, rosemary, and lemon zest, and cook for about 2 minutes, spooning the butter sauce over the salmon fillets occasionally.

6. Serve hot.

NUTRITION:

Calories: 301; Fat: 21.2g; Protein: 27.7g; Carbohydrates: 1.3g.

FRIDAY - DAY 26 - BREAKFAST
CHEESECAKE CUPS

PREPARATION TIME: 5 MINUTES | COOKING TIME: 0 MINUTES | SERVINGS: 4

INGREDIENTS:

8 ounces cream cheese, softened

2 ounces heavy cream

1 teaspoon Stevia Glycerite

1 teaspoon Splenda

1 teaspoon vanilla flavoring (Frontier Organic)

DIRECTIONS:

1. Combine all the ingredients.

2. Whip until a pudding consistency is achieved.

3. Divide into cups.

4. Refrigerate until served!

NUTRITION:

Calories: 205; Fat: 19g; Protein: 5g; Carbohydrates: 2g.

FRIDAY - DAY 26 - LUNCH
TUNA CAKES

PREPARATION TIME: 15 MINUTES | COOKING TIME: 10 MINUTES | SERVINGS: 2

INGREDIENTS:

1 (15-ounce) can water-packed tuna, drained

½ celery stalk, chopped

2 tablespoons fresh parsley, chopped

1 teaspoon fresh dill, chopped

2 tablespoons walnuts, chopped

2 tablespoons mayonnaise

1 organic egg, beaten

1 tablespoon butter

3 cups lettuce

DIRECTIONS:

1. Add all ingredients (except the butter and lettuce) in a bowl and mix until well-combined.
2. Make two equal-sized patties from the mixture.
3. Melt some butter and cook the patties for about 2-3 minutes.
4. Carefully flip the side and cook for about 2-3 minutes.
5. Divide the lettuce onto serving plates.
6. Top each plate with one burger and serve.

NUTRITION:

Calories: 267; Fat: 12.5g; Protein: 11.5g; Carbohydrates: 3.8g.

GREEK VEGGIE BRIAM

PREPARATION TIME: 10 MINUTES | COOKING TIME: 30 MINUTES | SERVINGS: 4

INGREDIENTS:

1/3 cup good-quality olive oil, divided

1 onion, thinly sliced

1 tablespoon minced garlic

¾ small eggplant, diced

2 zucchinis, diced

2 cups chopped cauliflower

1 red bell pepper, diced

2 cups diced tomatoes

2 tablespoons chopped fresh parsley

2 tablespoons chopped fresh oregano

Sea salt, for seasoning

Freshly ground black pepper, for seasoning

1 ½ cups crumbled feta cheese

¼ cup pumpkin seeds

DIRECTIONS:

1. Preheat the oven. Set the oven to broil and lightly grease a 9-by-13-inch casserole dish with olive oil.

2. Sauté the aromatics in a medium stockpot over medium heat, warm 3 tablespoons of the olive oil. Add the onion and garlic and sauté until they've softened, about 3 minutes.

3. Sauté the vegetables. Stir in the eggplant, cook, stirring occasionally.

4. Add the zucchini, cauliflower, and red bell pepper and cook for 5 minutes.

5. Stir in the tomatoes, parsley, and oregano and cook, stirring from time to time, until the vegetables are tender, about 10 minutes. Season it with salt and pepper.

6. Broil. Put vegetable mix in the casserole dish and top with the crumbled feta. Broil until the cheese is melted.

7. Serve. Divide the casserole between four plates and top it with the pumpkin seeds. Drizzle with the remaining olive oil.

NUTRITION:

Calories: 341; Fat: 5.1g; Protein: 1.4g; Carbohydrates: 1.2g.

STRAWBERRY SHAKE

PREPARATION TIME: 5 MINUTES | COOKING TIME: 0 MINUTES | SERVINGS: 1

INGREDIENTS:

¾ cup coconut milk (from the carton)

¼ cup heavy cream

7 ice cubes

2 tablespoons sugar-free strawberry Torani syrup

¼ teaspoon Xanthan Gum

DIRECTIONS:

1. Combine all the ingredients into blender.

2. Blend for 1-2 minutes.

3. Serve!

NUTRITION:

Calories: 270; Fat: 27g; Protein: 2.5g; Carbohydrates: 6.5g.

SATURDAY - DAY 27 - LUNCH
PIZZA BIANCA

PREPARATION TIME: 10 MINUTES | COOKING TIME: 10 MINUTES | SERVINGS: 2

INGREDIENTS:

2 tablespoons olive oil

4 eggs

2 tablespoons water

1 jalapeño pepper, diced

¼ cup mozzarella cheese, shredded

2 chives, chopped

2 cups egg Alfredo sauce

½ teaspoon oregano

½ cup mushrooms, sliced

DIRECTIONS:

1. Preheat oven to 360°F.

2. In a bowl, whisk eggs, water, and oregano. Heat the olive oil in a large skillet.

3. The egg mixture must be poured in, then let it cook until set, flipping once.

4. Remove and spread the Alfredo sauce and jalapeño pepper all over.

5. Top with mozzarella cheese, mushrooms and chives. Let it bake for 10 minutes

NUTRITION:

Calories: 314; Fat: 15.6g; Protein: 10.4g; Carbohydrates: 5.9g.

ROASTED TENDERLOIN

PREPARATION TIME: 10 MINUTES | COOKING TIME: 50 MINUTES | SERVINGS: 10

INGREDIENTS:

1 grass-fed beef tenderloin roast

4 garlic cloves

1 tablespoon rosemary

Salt

Ground black pepper

1 tablespoon olive oil

DIRECTIONS:

1. Warm-up oven to 425°F.

2. Place beef meat into the prepared roasting pan. Massage with garlic, rosemary, salt, and black pepper and oil. Roast the beef for 45-50 minutes.

3. Remove, cool, slice, and serve.

NUTRITION:

Calories: 295; Fat: 13.9g; Protein: 39.5g; Carbohydrates: 0.6g.

SUNDAY - DAY 28 - BREAKFAST
BACON HASH

PREPARATION TIME: 5 MINUTES | COOKING TIME: 10 MINUTES | SERVINGS: 2

INGREDIENTS:

1 small green pepper

2 jalapeno peppers

1 small onion

4 eggs

6 bacon slices

DIRECTIONS:

1. Chop the bacon into chunks using a food processor. Set aside for now. Slice the onions and peppers into thin strips. Dice the jalapenos as small as possible.

2. Heat a skillet and fry the veggies. Once browned, combine the ingredients and cook until crispy. Place on a serving dish with fried eggs.

NUTRITION:

Calories: 366; Fat: 24g; Protein: 23g; Carbohydrates: 9g.

TEMPURA ZUCCHINI WITH CREAM CHEESE DIP

PREPARATION TIME: 15 MINUTES | COOKING TIME: 15 MINUTES | SERVINGS: 4

INGREDIENTS:

Tempura zucchinis:

1 ½ cups (200g) almond flour

2 tablespoons heavy cream

1 teaspoon salt

2 tablespoons olive oil + extra for frying

1 ¼ cups (300ml) water

½ tablespoon sugar-free maple syrup

2 large zucchinis, cut into 1-inch thick strips

Cream cheese dip:

8 ounces cream cheese, room temperature

½ cup (113g) sour cream

1 teaspoon taco seasoning

1 scallion, chopped

1 green chili, deseeded and minced

DIRECTIONS:

1. In a bowl, mix the almond flour, heavy cream, salt, peanut oil, water, and maple syrup.

2. Dredge the zucchini strips in the mixture until well-coated.

3. Heat about four tablespoons of olive oil in a non-stick skillet.

4. Working in batches, use tongs to remove the zucchinis (draining extra liquid) into the oil.

5. Fry per side for 1 to 2 minutes and remove the zucchinis onto a paper towel-lined plate to drain grease.

6. In a bowl or container, mix the cream cheese, taco seasoning, sour cream, scallion, and green chili.

7. Serve the tempura zucchinis with the cream cheese dip.

NUTRITION:

Calories: 316; Fat: 8.4g; Protein: 5.1g; Carbohydrates: 4.1g.

CREAMY PARMESAN SHRIMP

PREPARATION TIME: 10 MINUTES | COOKING TIME: 20 MINUTES | SERVINGS: 4

INGREDIENTS:

1 ½ pounds shrimp

½ cup chicken stock

¼ teaspoon red pepper flakes

1 cup parmesan cheese, grated

1 cup fresh basil leaves

1 ½ cups heavy cream

¼ teaspoon paprika

3 ounces roasted red peppers, sliced

½ onion, minced

1 tablespoon garlic, minced

3 tablespoons butter

Pepper

Salt

DIRECTIONS:

1. Melt 2 tablespoons butter in a pan over medium heat.
2. Season shrimp with pepper and salt and sear in a pan for 1-2 minutes. Transfer shrimp on a plate.
3. Add remaining butter in a pan.
4. Add red chili flakes, paprika, roasted peppers, garlic, onion, pepper, and salt and cook for 5 minutes.
5. Add stock and stir well and cook until liquid reduced by half.
6. Turn heat to low, add cream and stir for 1-2 minutes.
7. Add basil and parmesan cheese and stir for 1-2 minutes.
8. Return shrimp to the pan and cook for 1-2 minutes.
9. Serve and enjoy.

NUTRITION:

Calories: 524; Fat: 33.2g; Protein: 47.8g; Carbohydrates: 8.3g.

CONCLUSION

Dealing with weight issues can be disheartening, and you do not have to be extremely over-weight or obese to feel the effects. These extra pounds can put a strain on your overall health and wellness. They can make you less efficient in your work life and everyday activities. They can take you away from the things you like to do and the places you love to visit. They can make you feel winded and out of breath at the simplest activities. They can take away your joy for living and living life to the fullest.

When people get older, their bones weaken. At 50, your bones are likely not as strong as they used to be; however, you can keep them in really good conditions. Consuming milk to give calcium cannot do enough to strengthen your bones. What you can do is to make use of the Keto diet as it is low in toxins. Toxins negatively affect the absorption of nutrients and so with this, your bones can take in all they need.

Whether you have met your weight loss goals, your life changes, or you simply want to eat whatever you want again. You cannot just suddenly start consuming Carbs again because it will shock your system. Have an idea of what you want to allow back into your consumption slowly. Be familiar with portion sizes and stick to that amount of Carbs for the first few times you eat post-keto.

Start with non-processed Carbs like whole grain, beans, and fruits. Start slow and see how your body reacts before resolving to add Carbs one meal at a time.

The things to watch out for when coming off keto are weight gain, bloating, and feeling hungry. The weight gain is nothing to freak out over; perhaps, you might not even gain any. It all depends on your diet, how your body processes carbs, and, of course, water weight. The length of your keto diet is a significant factor in how much weight you have lost, which is caused by the reduction of Carbs. The bloating will occur because of the reintroduction of fibrous foods and your body getting used to digesting them again. The bloating van lasts for a few days to a few weeks.

The ketogenic diet is the ultimate tool you can use to plan your future. Can you picture being more involved, more productive and efficient, and more relaxed and energetic? That future is possible for you, and it does not have to be a complicated process to achieve that vision. You can choose right now to be healthier and slimmer and more fulfilled tomorrow. It is possible with the ketogenic diet.

This is not a fancy diet that promises falsehoods of miracle weight loss. This diet is proven by years of science and research, which benefits not only your waistline, but your heart, skin, brain, and organs. It does not just improve your physical health but your mental and emotional health as well. This diet improves your health holistically.

KETO DIET COOKBOOK
FOR WOMEN OVER 50

A Simple Guide to a Healthy Lifestyle After Fifty.

Tasty and Easy Low-Carb Ketogenic Recipes to Lose Weight, Detox Your Body, and Balance Hormones

INTRODUCTION

Each of us is unique, which is why the most effective diet plan for any woman is one that is tailor-made to meet her personal needs. If you are to maximize your health and well-being you have to know how best to do this at your particular stage in life and in your particular situation.

The good news is that working out a health-care plan that matches the complexity of your life is not impossible. With a guide to follow and a mindset geared towards success, you'll be on your way to a healthier you in no time.

As we age, it becomes more imperative that we obtain as much information as possible in order to embrace a lifestyle that encourages good health and helps create a sense of well-being. Women over 50 have shown a great interest in gaining as much information as possible in order to sustain their current health and to make sensible choices about their lifestyles and behaviors. This natural curiosity helps us to acquire new eating habits and modify our exercise routines in order to ensure a more satisfying and longer life. We turn our attention to medical research on nutrition and nutritional needs in order to learn as much as possible about our own health and how to care for our bodies. The results are finally provided, it often seems as though the medical community is playing a game of Russian roulette and the findings seem to change like the seasons.

It can be frustrating when things you thought were right are turned inside-out as new findings come to light. One moment you are told to eat more carbohydrates, and the next you're told that carbohydrates are the cause of your excess weight. Knowledge from medical research usually builds up only slowly, and sometimes it changes completely as more information becomes available.

What you'll find here is information on how to create and maintain a healthy lifestyle. The keto diet has been around for a very long time and has been proved to be one of the most comprehensive eating plans to not only help you lose unwanted pounds but to help you create a life-long way of eating that will ensure the best of health for years to come.

THE SCIENCE BEHIND THE DIET

One of the toughest things to do when starting any diet is choosing which diet to start. There are literally hundreds of diets to choose from at any given time. Many of these diets make promises of all kinds including effortless weight loss without sacrifice and without hunger. They offer quick results with minimal effort. They share their gimmicks, tricks, and hooks to get you excited enough to begin, but fall short of explaining the science behind their promises. Usually, because there is no science. Just fad after fad that someone has thought up to make money. You know how their story ends. You start, you fall, and you fail. And you end up right back where you started, very often, having added a couple of extra pounds to top it all off.

The keto diet is much more than a fad diet; it will actually teach you a new way of eating that is not just for the time being, but forever. The science is flawless, the results have proven time and time again. It is a completely new way of eating that is not just for the moment—but is sustainable for a lifetime. You will be training your body to treat food in a whole new way.

The keto diet was originally developed by researchers and doctors for children with epilepsy. Studies proved that this special high-fat, very low-carb and protein plan helped to control, if not eliminate, seizures in children and adults with this debilitating disease. Over the course of the studies, it was noted that the patient's weights were affected in a positive way.

Let's take a moment and reflect on what we are actually talking about here. The word "diet" has such a negative connotation in today's world. It brings to mind images of celery sticks and carrots, starvation, and a never-ending struggle with will power. It implies that someone has issues with eating habits, most specifically, overeating. But that's not what the word should mean to us. If you check a dictionary, you'll find that the word diet is simply a reference to the type of foods that a person, community, or animal habitually eats.

Let's begin by embracing the idea that the keto diet is not really a "diet" at all, but merely a habitual way of eating to create a healthy body. We aren't going to "restrict" our foods, we may eliminate some, and we may control portions on others, but we will not think of our new-way-of-eating as depriving ourselves—but instead, that we are creating a pathway to a healthier and happy body, and consider this new-way-of-eating as the right path to lead us towards that goal.

WHAT IS KETO DIET?

As you'd probably already know, the ketogenic diet is a low-carb diet where you eliminate or minimize carbohydrate intake. Proteins and fats replace the extra carbs while you cut back on pastries and sugar.

HOW DOES IT WORK?

See, when you consume less than 50 grams of carbs per day, your body starts to run out of blood sugar (which is used as fuel to provide your body quick energy). Once there are no sugar reserves left, your body will start to utilize fat and protein for energy. This entire process is known as ketosis, and this is exactly what helps you lose weight.

GETTING INTO KETOSIS

The process of ketosis is named after the byproduct, which is produced along with energy when a fat molecule is broken down. It is known as a ketone. When a person switches to the ketogenic approach, his body too switches to ketosis to meet the energy needs. It metabolizes fats and produces more ketones than usual. These ketones are mainly responsible for decreasing the oxidative stress of the body and detoxify the mind and body. Thus, ketosis works in three ways: by reducing the carb intake, it controls weight gain; then it provides energy through the breakdown of fats, which is more lasting; and finally, through the release of ketones, it regulates improved metabolism.

SIGNS THAT YOU ARE IN KETOSIS

Since the human body heavily depends on carbs, it always takes time for the body to adapt to the new ketogenic lifestyle. It's like changing the fuel of a machine when the body is switched to the ketogenic diet; it shows some different signs than usual, which are as follows:

Increased Urination

Ketones are normally known as a diuretic, which means that they help remove the extra water out of the body through increased urination. So high levels of ketones mean more urination than normal. Due to ketosis, more acetoacetate is released about three times faster than usual, which is excreted along with urine, and its release then causes more urination.

Dry Mouth

It is obvious that more urination means the loss of high amounts of water, which causes dehydration as more water is released out of the body due to ketosis. Along with those fluids, many metabolites and electrolytes are also excreted out of the body. Therefore, it is always recommended to increase the water consumption on a ketogenic diet, along with a good intake of electrolytes, to maintain the water levels of the body.

Bad Breath

A ketone, which is known as acetone, is released through our breath. This ketone has a distinct smell, and it takes some time to go away. Due to ketosis, a high number of acetones are released through the breath, which causes bad breath.

Reduced Appetite and Lasting Energy

This is the clearest sign of ketosis. Since fat molecules are high-energy macronutrients, each molecule is broken down to produce three times more energy than a carb molecule. Therefore, a person feels more energized round the clock.

WHY SHOULD YOU SWITCH TO KETO?

Once you start to hit 50, you likely don't indulge in strenuous activities anymore, so your body will need fewer calories to function. This is when you should start eliminating added sugars from your diet. Plus, a low-carb diet that is rich in healthy vegetables and meat will prove to be far better for people suffering from insulin insensitivity and your overall health. Hence, start reading food labels more often and opt for healthier options.

Compared to other diets, keto has a better chance of helping you lose weight more quickly. The diet is also incredibly popular as you're not encouraged to starve yourself. It would help if you worked towards a more high-fat and protein diet, which isn't as difficult as counting calories. A recent study from the Hebrew University of Jerusalem has indicated how eating a diet rich in healthy fats can help you lose weight in the long-term.

Therefore, the ketogenic diet prescribes the use of fat-rich substances, like all vegetable oils, nut oils, cheese, cream cheese, butter, and creams. On the other hand, it restricts the daily carb intake to only 50 grams or less. On a ketogenic diet, a person must avoid the intake of grains, legumes, starchy vegetables, high-sugar fruits, sugars, sugary beverages and drinks, and all other products containing these basic items. These ingredients must be replaced with non-starchy vegetables, sugar-free products, meat, seafood, nut-based milk and processed dairy items.

MACRONUTRIENTS AND KETO

The food you consume provides nutrition to the body. Various types of nutrients are present in the food. They are broadly classified into macronutrients and micronutrients. Macronutrients are those nutrients required in significant quantities in the food to provide necessary energy and raw material to build different body parts. These are:

- Carbohydrates
- Proteins
- Fats

CARBOHYDRATES

Carbohydrates are important energy sources of the body. In a Keto diet plan, you have to cut on your carbs to eliminate this energy source and compel your body to spend the already present food stores in your body. These food stores are present as fat in your body. Once your body turns to these fat deposits for energy, you start to lose weight.

Carbohydrates should not constitute more than 5–10% of your daily caloric intake.

Carbohydrates are present in a variety of foods. You should make sure that the small quota of carbohydrates you can consume comes from healthy carbohydrate sources like low-carb vegetables and fruits, e.g., broccoli, lemon, and tomatoes.

PROTEINS

Proteins are really important because they provide subunits, which are building blocks of the body. They produce various hormones, muscles, enzymes, and other working machinery of the body. They provide energy to the body as well.

No more than 20-25% of your daily caloric intake should come from proteins. As a rule of thumb, a healthy person should consume about 0.5-0.7 grams of proteins per pound of total body weight.

Many people make a mistake in a keto diet consuming much more protein than they should. This not only puts additional strain on their kidneys, but is also very unhealthy for the digestive system.

Eat a good variety of proteins from various sources like tofu, fish, chicken, and other white meat sources, including seeds, nuts, eggs, and dairy (though you shouldn't fill your diet with cheese). Red meat like beef can be enjoyed less frequently. We also suggest you avoid processed meats, which are typically laden with artificial preservatives.

Processed meat refers to meat that's modified through a series of processes, which might include salting, smoking, canning, and, most importantly, treated with preservatives. Such variants typically include sausages, jerky, and salami. As these meats are not even considered healthy for normal diets, we suggest limiting your portions to only once or twice a week.

FATS

In keto, fats serve as the mainstay of your diet. It seems counterintuitive to consume what you want to eliminate from your body, but that is exactly how this strategy works. But before you go about loading your body with all types of fats, keep the following things in your mind:

1. You have to cut on carbs before this high-fat diet can be of any benefit to the body.

2. Fats should take up about 70-75% of your daily caloric intake.

3. Fats are of various types, and you have to be aware of the kind of fats you should consume.

Dietary fats can be divided into two kinds: healthy and harmful. Unsaturated fats belong to the healthier group, whereas saturated and trans-unsaturated fats belong to the unhealthier category. Aside from the differences in their health effects, these fats essentially differ in terms of chemical structure and bonding.

Saturated Fats

Saturated fats drive up cholesterol levels and contain harmful LDL cholesterol that can clog arteries anywhere in the body, especially the heart, and increase the risk of cardiovascular diseases. These fats are mainly contained in animal origin (except fish, which contains a small part). They are also present in plant-based foods, such as coconut oil. However, coconut oil contains medium-chain fatty acids, which are saturated fats different from animal origin, and therefore considered a healthy food.

Trans Fats

Trans fats, or trans-fatty acids, are a particular form of unsaturated fat. These unhealthy fats are manufactured through a partial hydrogenation food process. Moreover, some studies differentiate the health risks of those obtained industrially or transformed by cooking, from those naturally present in food (for example, vaccenic acid); the latter would be harmless or even beneficial to health.

The industrial foods that contain these hydrogenated fats are mainly: fried foods (especially French fries), margarine, microwave popcorn, brioche, sweet snacks, and pretzels.

While these foods may taste good, they're an unhealthy kind of fat and should be avoided.

Trans fats are known to increase unhealthy cholesterol levels in the blood, thus increasing the risks of cardiovascular disease.

Unsaturated Fats

These "good fats" contain healthy cholesterol. Unsaturated fats can most commonly be found in nuts, veggies, and fish. These fats keep your heart healthy and are a good substitution for saturated fats.

AGING AND NUTRITIONAL NEEDS

At any age, proper nutrition is incredibly important, but as we age, our bodies are going through some major changes. To help with these changes, it will be essential to make certain adjustments to our routines and nutrition. The vital factor to remember is that it is never too late to start taking care of yourself. When you neglect your health after the age of fifty, the effects may become more noticeable than ever before. So, how exactly does age affect our nutritional needs?

As we age, you can expect a number of different changes to happen in your body, including thinner skin, loss of muscle, and less stomach acid. When these things happen, this can, unfortunately, make you more prone to nutrient deficiencies and overall quality of life. This is where the Ketogenic Diet comes in handy! By eating a variety of foods and incorporating the proper supplements, you will be able to meet your nutrient needs with no issues! Below, you will find some of the effects of aging and how to help the issue.

Less Calories—More Nutrients

On a general basis, an individual's daily calorie count will depend on a number of factors, including activity level, muscle mass, weight, and height. In order to maintain or lose weight, we will need to begin lowering the number of calories we take in. Generally, older adults tend to exercise and move less compared to younger individuals.

While consuming fewer calories, it is important to continue getting higher levels of nutrients. For this reason, it is highly suggested to consume a variety of foods such as low-carb vegetables and lean meats to help get the proper nutrients and fight against any nutrient deficiencies. The nutrients you will want to focus on include vitamin B12, calcium, and vitamin D, Magnesium, Potassium, Omega-3, fatty acids, and Iron.

Benefits of Fiber

While many people do not like to discuss this, constipation is a prevalent health issue for individuals over the age of 50. In fact, women over the age of 65 are two to three times more likely to experience constipation! This may be due to the fact that people over the age of 50 generally move less and are more likely to be taking a medication that has constipation as an unfortunate side effect.

To help relieve constipation, you will want to make sure you are getting enough fiber. When you eat more fiber, it is able to pass through your gut, undigested, and help regulate bowel movements and form stool. As an added benefit, high-fiber diets may also be able to prevent diverticular disease. Diverticular disease is a condition where small pouches build along the wall of the colon and become inflamed.

Focus on Protein

As we age, it is very common to lose both strength and muscle. In fact, on average, an adult will lose anywhere between 3-8% of their muscle mass per decade after the age of 30. When we lose muscle mass, it could lead to poor health, fractures, and weakness among the elderly population. By eating more protein, you can help fight sarcopenia and maintain your muscle mass.

Vitamin B12

As mentioned earlier, keeping up with proper nutrients is going to be vital for your health. One of the vitamins you will want to focus on is Vitamin B12. This is a water-soluble vitamin that is in charge of making red blood cells and keeping your brain healthy. Unfortunately, it is estimated that anywhere from 1-30% of individuals over the age of 50 have a lowered ability to absorb this vitamin from their diet.

One of the main reasons individuals over the age of 50 have difficulty absorbing vitamin B12 may be due to the fact that they have reduced stomach acid reduction. Vitamin B12 is bound to proteins. In order for your body to use this vitamin, the stomach acid separates it from the protein and becomes absorbed. To benefit your new diet, you will want to consider taking a supplement of vitamin B12 or consuming foods that are fortified with the vitamin.

Vitamin D and Calcium

When it comes to bone health, calcium and vitamin D are going to be very important. While calcium is in charge of maintaining and building healthy bones, it depends on vitamin D to help the body absorb the calcium in the first place! Unfortunately, adults have a harder time absorbing calcium in their diets. This may be due to the fact that the gut absorbs less calcium as we age. However, the main culprit of a reduction in calcium is typically due to a vitamin D deficiency. As you can tell, they work hand in hand!

The reason we may experience a vitamin D deficiency is due to thinning skin. Generally, our body makes vitamin D from the cholesterol in the skin when it is exposed to sunlight. As the skin becomes thinner, it reduces the ability to make vitamin D and, in turn, reduces the ability to get enough calcium. When these two things happen, it increases the risk of fractures and bone loss.

To help counter this aging effect, you will want to make sure you are getting enough vitamin D and calcium in your diet. Some accessible sources will be dairy products, leafy vegetables, and dark greens. As far as Vitamin D goes, you will want to include a variety of fish or even a Vitamin D supplement such as cod liver oil.

Dehydration

On the Ketogenic Diet or not, staying hydrated is important at any age. In fact, water makes up about 60% of our bodies! Whether you are 20, 30, or 50, the body still continually loses water through urine and sweat. As we age, it makes us more prone to dehydration.

When we become dehydrated, the water detects the thirst through receptors found all throughout the body and the brain. As we age, the receptors become less sensitive, making it hard to distinguish the thirst in the first place. On top of this, our kidneys are there to help converse water, but they also lose function with age.

Unfortunately, the consequences of dehydration are pretty harsh for the older population. When you are dehydrated long-term, this could reduce your ability to absorb medication and could worsen any medical condition. For this reason, it will be vital you keep up with your intake of water. I suggest trying a water challenge with friends and family or try having a glass of water with each meal you have.

Appetite

The last topic we will tackle is the decrease in appetite. While this may seem like a benefit, a lack of eating could lead to a number of different nutritional deficiencies and unwanted weight loss. Poor appetite is most commonly linked to poor health.

It is believed that some of the significant factors behind appetite loss could be due to changes in smell, taste, and hormones. Generally, older adults who have lower levels of hunger have higher levels of fullness hormones. When this happens, it causes individuals to be less hungry overall. As we age, the changes in smell and taste can also make food seem less appealing.

If you find this happens to you, you may want to establish a healthy habit of snacking. When you snack, try to reach for keto-friendly foods such as eggs, and almonds to help put the nutrients back into your diet. If you are aware of this issue, it is something you can get a grasp on before it becomes a real problem.

IMPORTANT HEALTH TIPS AFTER 50

Nobody told you that life was going to be this way! But don't worry. There's still plenty of time to make amendments and take care of your health. Here are a couple of tips that will allow you to lead a healthier life in your fifties:

START BUILDING ON IMMUNITY

Every day, our body is exposed to free radicals and toxins from the environment. The added stress of work and family problems doesn't make it any easier for us. To combat this, you must start consuming healthy veggies that contain plenty of antioxidants and build a healthier immune system.

This helps ward off unwanted illnesses and diseases, allowing you to maintain good health.

Adding healthier veggies to your keto diet will help you obtain various minerals, vitamins, and antioxidants.

CONSIDER QUITTING SMOKING

It's never too late to try to quit smoking, even if you are in your fifties. Once a smoker begins to quit, the body quickly starts to heal the previous damages caused by smoking.

Once you start quitting, you'll notice how you'll be able to breathe easier while acquiring a better sense of smell and taste. Over a period of time, eliminating the habit of smoking can greatly reduce the risks of high blood pressure, strokes, and heart attack. Please note how these diseases are much more common among people in the fifties and above than in younger people.

Not to mention, quitting smoking will help you stay more active and enjoy better health with your friends and family.

STAY SOCIAL

Aging can be a daunting process, and trying to get through it all on your own isn't particularly helpful. We recommend you to stay in touch with friends and family or become a part of a local community club or network. Some older people find it comforting to get an emotional support animal.

Being surrounded by people you love will give you a sense of belonging and will improve your mood. It'll also keep your mind and memory sharp as you engage in different conversations.

HEALTH SCREENINGS YOU SHOULD GET AFTER YOUR FIFTIES

Don't let the joy of these years be robbed away from you because of poor health. Getting simple tests done can go a long way in identifying any potential health problems that you may have. Here is a list of health screenings you should get done:

Check Your Blood Pressure

Your blood pressure is a reliable indicator of your heart health. In simple words, blood pressure is a measure of how fast blood travels through the artery walls. Very high or even very low blood pressure can be a sign of an underlying problem. Once you reach your 50s, you should have your blood pressure checked more often.

EKG

The EKG reveals your heart health and activity. Short for electrocardiogram, the EKG helps identify problems in the heart. The process works by highlighting any rhythm problems that may be in the heart, such as poor heart muscles, improper blood flow, or any other form of abnormality. Getting an EKG is also a predictive measure for understanding the chances of a heart attack. Since people starting their fifties are at greater risk of getting a heart attack, you should get yourself checked more often.

Mammogram

Mammograms help rule out the risks of breast cancer. Women who enter their fifties should ideally get a mammogram every two years. If you have a family history, getting one becomes especially important.

Blood Sugar Levels

If you're somebody who used to grab a fast food meal every once in a while before you switched to keto, then you should definitely check your blood sugar levels more carefully. Blood sugar levels indicate whether or not you have diabetes. And you know how the saying goes, "prevention is better than cure." It's best to clear these possibilities out of the way sooner than later.

Check for Osteoporosis

Unfortunately, as you grow older, you also become susceptible to a number of bone diseases. Osteoporosis is a bone-related condition in which bones begin to lose mass, becoming frail and weak. Owing to this, seniors become more prone to fractures. This can make even the smallest of falls detrimental to your health.

Annual Physical Exam

Your insurance must be providing coverage for your annual physical exam. So, there's no reason why you should not take advantage of it. This checkup helps identify the state of your health. You'll probably be surprised by how much doctors can tell from a single blood test.

Eye Exam

As you start to aging, you'll notice how your eyesight will start to deteriorate. It's quite likely that vision is not as sharp as it used to be. Ideally, you should have gotten your first eye exam during your 40s, but it isn't too late. Get one as soon as possible to prevent symptoms from escalating.

Be Wary Of Any Weird Moles

While skin cancer can become a problem at any age, older adults should pay closer attention to any moles or unusual skin tags in their bodies. While most cancers can be easily treated, melanoma can be particularly quite dangerous. If you have noticed any recent moles in your body that have changed in color, size, or shape, make sure to visit the dermatologist.

Check Your Cholesterol Levels

High cholesterol levels can be dangerous to your health and can be an indicator of many diseases. Things become more complicated for conditions that don't show particular symptoms. Your total cholesterol levels should be below 200 mg per deciliter just to be on the safe side. Your doctor will take a simple blood test and will give you a couple of guidelines with the results. In case there is something to be worried about, you should make serious dietary and lifestyle changes.

KETOGENIC DIET AND MENOPAUSE

There comes an age in a woman's life where her menstrual cycle will finally end. This is when your ovaries stop releasing eggs, better known as ovulation, and therefore menstruation ends. This condition is generally observed in women above the age of 50. There is no defined age that shows when a woman can expect menopause.

There are times where women may experience menopause prematurely as well. This happens if a woman has undergone surgeries like hysterectomy (surgery that involves the removal of ovaries). It can also happen from any injuries that may have caused damage to the ovaries. If this happens before the age of 50, it is classified as premature menopause.

Menopause, as harmless as it sounds, can be quite a troubling phase for women. The hot flashes you experience will keep you up at night, with an elevated heartbeat. The constant feeling of being irritated and a clear downfall in your sex life can contribute greatly towards you feeling more and more grumpy.

Menopause takes a toll on your hormonal balance and the newly developed imbalance then pushes your body to gain massive weight, experience mood swings like never before, and a libido that is crashing faster than you can imagine.

If you think this is bad, here are some other issues that menopause can lead to:

- Chronic stress
- Anxiety
- Insulin spike
- Type 2 diabetes
- Heart diseases
- Polycystic Ovarian Syndrome (PCOS)

The overall picture, then, is grim! Fortunately, a difference in lifestyle and a carefully thought-out diet plan can change all that for you. I am not saying it happens overnight or within a week, but the profound impacts are felt rather quickly. In the longer run, keto will rescue you and your body from impending doom and allow you to lead a life without worrying about keeping a glucose monitor or any of the typical health-related equipment near you.

The keto diet, while there are many classes of it, helps your hormones be balanced. This means that you do not have to worry about insulin or any other hormones, hence minimizing the hot flashes and other symptoms. Even if they occur, they will be minor and far less painful.

Moreover, the keto diet jump-starts your sex drive. The fat-rich diet improves fat-soluble vitamin absorption. Not to forget, it especially helps with vitamin D, a vital micronutrient that goes missing with age. All in all, this provides all the drive you need to have intimate moments even in your fifties.

Heart Diseases

Keto diets help women over 50 to shed those extra pounds. Reducing any amount of weight greatly reduces the chances of a heart attack or any other heart complications. Through a carefully selected diet routine, not only are you losing weight and enjoying scrumptious meals, but you are significantly boosting your heart's health and reviving yourself from the otherwise dull state that you may have been in before.

Diabetes Control

Needless to say, the careful selection of ingredients, when cooked together, provide nutrition that is free from any processed or harmful contents such as sugar. Add this to the fact that keto automatically controls your insulin levels. The result is a glucose level that is always under control and continued control would lead to a day where you will say goodbye to the medications you might be taking for diabetes.

And so Much More!

By taking up the challenge and adapting the keto way, you are ensuring yourself one of the safest journeys into the older years, if not the safest of the lot. Sure, there will be days where you may miss a type of food or two, but that craving will be overshadowed by the benefits the keto diet will bring you.

With the help of the keto diet, you can expect a few more benefits such as:

- Improved and stable blood pressure levels
- A deeper sleep for those suffering from insomnia
- Improved kidney function
- More energy that lasts all day
- Improved bodily functions

THREE CHEESE EGG MUFFINS

PREPARATION TIME: 5 MINUTES | COOKING TIME: 20 MINUTES | SERVINGS: 12

INGREDIENTS:

1 tablespoon butter

½ cup diced yellow onion

12 large eggs, whisked

¼ cup cooked bacon, chopped

½ cup canned coconut milk

¼ cup sliced green onion

Salt and pepper

½ cup shredded cheddar cheese

½ cup shredded Swiss cheese

¼ cup grated parmesan cheese

DIRECTIONS:

1. Preheat the oven to 350°F and grease the cooking spray into a muffin pan.
2. Melt the butter over moderate heat in a medium skillet.
3. Add the onions, then cook until softened for 3 to 4 minutes.
4. Divide the mix between cups of muffins.
5. Whisk the bacon, coconut milk, green onions, salt, and pepper together and then spoon into the muffin cups.
6. In a cup, mix the three kinds of cheese and scatter over the egg muffins.
7. Bake till the egg is set, for 20 to 25 minutes.

NUTRITION:

Calories. 150; Fat: 11.6g; Protein: 10g; Carbohydrates: 2g.

BACON APPETIZERS

PREPARATION TIME: 15 MINUTES | COOKING TIME: 2 HOURS | SERVINGS: 6

INGREDIENTS:

1 pack Keto crackers

¾ cup Parmesan cheese, grated

1 pound bacon, sliced thinly

DIRECTIONS:

1. Preheat your oven to 250°F.
2. Arrange the crackers on a baking sheet.
3. Sprinkle cheese on top of each cracker.
4. Wrap each cracker with the bacon.
5. Bake in the oven for 2 hours.

NUTRITION:

Calories: 440; Fat: 33.4g; Protein: 29.4g; Carbohydrates: 3.7g.

MORNING COFFEE WITH CREAM

PREPARATION TIME: 0 MINUTES | COOKING TIME: 5 MINUTES | SERVINGS: 1

INGREDIENTS:

¾ cup coffee

¼ cup whipping cream

DIRECTIONS:

1. Make your favorite coffee.
2. Pour the heavy cream in a small saucepan and heat slowly until you get a frothy texture.
3. Pour the hot cream in a big cup, add coffee and enjoy your morning drink.

NUTRITION:

Calories: 202; Fat: 21g; Protein: 2g; Carbohydrates: 2g.

ANTIPASTI SKEWERS

PREPARATION TIME: 10 MINUTES | COOKING TIME: 0 MINUTE | SERVINGS: 6

INGREDIENTS:

6 small mozzarella balls

1 tablespoon olive oil

Salt to taste

1/8 teaspoon dried oregano

2 roasted yellow peppers, sliced into strips and rolled

6 cherry tomatoes

6 green olives, pitted

6 Kalamata olives, pitted

2 artichoke hearts, sliced into wedges

6 slices bacon, rolled

6 leaves fresh basil

DIRECTIONS:

1. Toss the mozzarella balls in olive oil.
2. Season with salt and oregano.
3. Thread the mozzarella balls and the rest of the ingredients into skewers.
4. Serve on a platter.

NUTRITION:

Calories: 180; Fat: 11.8g; Protein: 9.2g; Carbohydrates: 11.7g.

JALAPENO POPPERS

PREPARATION TIME: 30 MINUTES | COOKING TIME: 60 MINUTES | SERVINGS: 10

INGREDIENTS:

5 fresh jalapenos, sliced and seeded

4 ounces package cream cheese

¼ pound bacon, sliced in half

DIRECTIONS:

1. Preheat your oven to 275°F.

2. Place a wire rack over your baking sheet.

3. Stuff each jalapeno with cream cheese and wrap in bacon.

4. Secure with a toothpick.

5. Place on the baking sheet.

6. Bake for 1 hour and 15 minutes.

NUTRITION:

Calories: 103; Fat: 4.1g; Protein: 5.2g; Carbohydrates: 0.9g.

EGGS BENEDICT DEVILED EGGS

PREPARATION TIME: 15 MINUTES | COOKING TIME: 25 MINUTES | SERVINGS: 16

INGREDIENTS:

8 hardboiled eggs, sliced in half

1 tablespoon lemon juice

½ teaspoon mustard powder

1 pack Hollandaise sauce mix, prepared according to direction on the packaging

1 pound asparagus, trimmed and steamed

4 ounces bacon, cooked and chopped

DIRECTIONS:

1. Scoop out the egg yolks.
2. Mix the egg yolks with lemon juice, mustard powder and 1/3 cup of the Hollandaise sauce.
3. Spoon the egg yolk mixture into each of the egg whites.
4. Arrange the asparagus spears on a serving plate.
5. Top with the deviled eggs.
6. Sprinkle remaining sauce and bacon on top.

NUTRITION:

Calories: 80; Fat: 5.3g; Protein: 6.2g; Carbohydrates: 2.1g.

KETO BREAKFAST CHEESECAKE

PREPARATION TIME: 20 MINUTES | COOKING TIME: 45 MINUTES | SERVINGS: 24 MINI CHEESECAKES

INGREDIENTS:

Toppings:

¼ cup mixed berries for each cheesecake, frozen and thawed

For filling:

½ teaspoon vanilla extract

½ teaspoon almond extract

¾ cup sweetener

6 eggs

8 ounces cream cheese

16 ounces cottage cheese

For crust:

4 tablespoons salted butter

2 tablespoons sweetener

2 cups almonds, whole

DIRECTIONS:

1. Preheat oven to around 350°F.

2. Pulse almonds in a food processor, then add in butter and sweetener.

3. Pulse until all the ingredients mix well and a coarse dough forms.

4. Coat twelve silicone muffin pans using foil or paper liners.

5. Divide the batter evenly between the muffin pans, then press into the bottom part until it forms a crust and bakes for about 8 minutes.

6. In the meantime, mix the cream cheese and cottage cheese in a food processor, then pulse until the mixture is smooth.

7. Put in the extracts and sweetener, then combine until well mixed.

8. Add in eggs and pulse again until it becomes smooth; you might need to scrape down the mixture from the sides of the processor. Share the batter equally between the muffin pans, then bake for around 30-40 minutes until the middle is not wobbly when you shake the muffin pan lightly.

9. Put aside until cooled completely, then put in the refrigerator for about 2 hours and top with frozen and thawed berries.

NUTRITION:

Calories: 152; Fat: 12g; Protein: 6g; Carbohydrates: 3g.

EGG-CRUST PIZZA

PREPARATION TIME: 5 MINUTES | COOKING TIME: 15 MINUTES | SERVINGS: 1-2

INGREDIENTS:

¼ teaspoon dried oregano to taste

½ teaspoon spike seasoning to taste

1 ounce mozzarella, chopped into small cubes

6-8 sliced thinly black olives

6 slices turkey pepperoni, sliced in half

4-5 thinly sliced small grape tomatoes

2 eggs, beaten well

1-2 teaspoons olive oil

DIRECTIONS:

1. Preheat the broiler in an oven, then beat the eggs well in a small bowl. Cut the pepperoni and tomatoes in slices, then cut the mozzarella cheese into cubes.

2. Put some olive oil in a skillet over medium heat, then heat the pan for around one minute until it begins to get hot. Add in eggs and season with oregano and spike seasoning, then cook for around 2 minutes until the eggs begin to set at the bottom.

3. Drizzle half of the mozzarella, olives, pepperoni, and tomatoes on the eggs, followed by another layer of the remaining half of the above ingredients. Ensure that there is a lot of cheese on the topmost layers. Cover the skillet using a lid and cook until the cheese begins to melt and the eggs are set, for around 3-4 minutes.

4. Place the pan under the preheated broiler and cook until the top has browned and the cheese has melted nicely for around 2-3 minutes. Serve immediately.

NUTRITION:

Calories: 363; Fat: 24.1g; Protein: 19.25g; Carbohydrates: 20.8g.

BASIC OPIE ROLLS

PREPARATION TIME: 20 MINUTES | COOKING TIME: 35 MINUTES | SERVINGS: 12 ROLLS

INGREDIENTS:

1/8 teaspoon salt

1/8 teaspoon cream of tartar

3 ounces cream cheese

3 large eggs

DIRECTIONS:

1. Preheat the oven to about 300°F, then separate the egg whites from egg yolks and place both eggs in different bowls. Using an electric mixer, beat the egg whites well until the mixture is very bubbly, then add in the cream of tartar and mix again until it forms a stiff peak.

2. In the bowl with the egg yolks, put in 3 ounces of cubed cheese and salt. Mix well until the mixture has doubled in size and is pale yellow. Put the egg white mixture into the egg yolk mixture, then fold the mixture gently together.

3. Spray some oil on the cookie sheet coated with some parchment paper, then add dollops of the batter and bake for around 30 minutes.

4. You will know they are ready when the upper part of the rolls are firm and golden. Leave them to cool for a few minutes on a wire rack. Enjoy with some coffee.

NUTRITION:

Calories: 43; Fat: 3.7g; Protein: 2.1g; Carbohydrates: 0.3g.

SMOOTHIES RECIPES

CELERY JUICE

PREPARATION TIME: 10 MINUTES | COOKING TIME: 0 MINUTES | SERVINGS: 2

INGREDIENTS:

8 celery stalks with leaves

2 tablespoons fresh ginger, peeled

1 lemon, peeled

½ cup of filtered water

Pinch of salt

DIRECTIONS:

1. Place all the ingredients in a blender and pulse until well combined.

2. Through a fine mesh strainer, strain the juice and transfer it into 2 glasses.

3. Serve immediately.

NUTRITION:

Calories: 32; Fat: 1.1g; Protein: 1.2g; Carbohydrates: 1.3g.

GRAPEFRUIT & CELERY BLAST

PREPARATION TIME: 10 MINUTES | COOKING TIME: 0 MINUTES | SERVINGS: 1

INGREDIENTS:

1 grapefruit, peeled

2 stalks of celery

2 ounces kale

½ teaspoon matcha powder

DIRECTIONS:

1. Place ingredients into a blender with water to cover them and blitz until smooth.

NUTRITION:

Calories: 129; Fat: 2.1g; Protein: 1.2g; Carbohydrates: 12.1g.

LEMONY GREEN JUICE

PREPARATION TIME: 10 MINUTES | COOKING TIME: 0 MINUTES | SERVINGS: 2

INGREDIENTS:

2 large green apples, cored and sliced

4 cups fresh kale leaves

4 tablespoons fresh parsley leaves

1 tablespoon fresh ginger, peeled

1 lemon, peeled

½ cup of filtered water

Pinch of salt

DIRECTIONS:

1. Place all the ingredients in a blender and pulse until well combined.

2. Through a fine mesh strainer, strain the juice and transfer it into 2 glasses.

3. Serve immediately.

NUTRITION:

Calories: 196; Fat: 1.1g; Protein: 1.5g; Carbohydrates: 1.6g.

CHOCOLATE SEA SALT SMOOTHIE

PREPARATION TIME: 15 MINUTES | COOKING TIME: 0 MINUTES | SERVINGS: 2

INGREDIENTS:

1 avocado

2 cups almond milk

1 tablespoon tahini

¼ cup of cocoa powder

1 scoop Keto chocolate base

DIRECTIONS:

1. Combine all the fixing in a high-speed blender. Add ice and serve!

NUTRITION:

Calories: 235; Fat: 20g; Protein: 5.5g; Carbohydrates: 11.25g.

ORANGE & CELERY CRUSH

PREPARATION TIME: 10 MINUTES | COOKING TIME: 0 MINUTES | SERVINGS: 1

INGREDIENTS:

1 carrot, peeled

Stalks of celery

1 orange, peeled

½ teaspoon matcha powder

Juice of 1 lime

DIRECTIONS:

1. Place ingredients into a blender with enough water to cover them and blitz until smooth.

NUTRITION:

Calories: 150; Fat: 2.1g; Protein: 1.4g; Carbohydrates: 11.2g.

CREAMY STRAWBERRY & CHERRY SMOOTHIE

PREPARATION TIME: 10 MINUTES | COOKING TIME: 0 MINUTES | SERVINGS: 1

INGREDIENTS:

3 ½ ounces strawberries

1 ounce of frozen pitted cherries

1 tablespoon Greek yogurt

1 ounce of unsweetened soya milk

DIRECTIONS:

1. Place the ingredients into a blender then process until smooth.

2. Serve and enjoy.

NUTRITION:

Calories: 203; Fat: 3.1g; Protein: 1.7g; Carbohydrates: 9g

ROSEMARY CHEESE CHIPS WITH GUACAMOLE

PREPARATION TIME: 10 MINUTES | COOKING TIME: 20 MINUTES | SERVINGS: 4

INGREDIENTS:

1 tablespoon rosemary

1 cup Grana Padano, grated

¼ teaspoon sweet paprika

¼ teaspoon garlic powder

2 avocados, pitted and scooped

1 tomato, chopped

DIRECTIONS:

1. Preheat oven to 350°F and line a baking sheet with parchment paper. Mix Grana Padano cheese, paprika, rosemary, and garlic powder evenly.

2. Spoon 6-8 teaspoons on the baking sheet creating spaces between each mound.

3. Flatten mounds. Bake for 5 minutes, cool, and remove to a plate. To make the guacamole, mash avocado, with a fork in a bowl, add in tomato, and continue to mash until mostly smooth. Season with salt.

4. Serve crackers with guacamole.

NUTRITION:

Calories: 229; Fat: 20g; Protein: 10g; Carbohydrates: 2,6g

BAKED CHORIZO WITH COTTAGE CHEESE

PREPARATION TIME: 10 MINUTES | COOKING TIME: 30 MINUTES | SERVINGS: 6

INGREDIENTS:

7 ounces Spanish chorizo, sliced

4 ounces cottage cheese, pureed

¼ cup chopped parsley

DIRECTIONS:

1. Preheat the oven to 325°F. Line a baking dish with waxed paper. Bake the chorizo for minutes until crispy. Remove from the oven and let cool.

2. Arrange on a Serves platter. Top each slice with cottage cheese and parsley.

NUTRITION:

Calories: 172; Fat: 13g; Protein: 5g; Carbohydrates: 0.52g.

CRISPY CHORIZO WITH CHEESY TOPPING

PREPARATION TIME: 10 MINUTES | COOKING TIME: 30 MINUTES | SERVINGS: 6

INGREDIENTS:

7 ounces Spanish chorizo, sliced

4 ounces cream cheese

¼ cup chopped parsley

DIRECTIONS:

1. Preheat oven to 325°F. Line a baking dish with waxed paper. Bake chorizo for minutes until crispy. Remove and let cool.

2. Arrange on a serving platter. Top with cream cheese.

3. Serve sprinkled with parsley.

NUTRITION:

Calories: 172; Fat: 13g; Protein: 5g; Carbohydrates. 3.3g.

GOLDEN CHEESE CRISPS

PREPARATION TIME: 10 MINUTES | COOKING TIME: 10 MINUTES | SERVINGS: 4

INGREDIENTS:

1 cup Edam cheese

1 cup provolone cheese

1/3 teaspoon dried oregano

1/3 teaspoon dried rosemary

½ teaspoon garlic powder

1/3 teaspoon dried basil

DIRECTIONS:

1. Preheat your oven to 390°F.

2. In a small bowl mix the dried oregano, rosemary, basil, and garlic powder. Set aside. Combine the Edam cheese and provolone cheese in another medium bowl.

3. Line a large baking dish with parchment paper, place tablespoon-sized stacks of the cheese mixture on the baking dish. Sprinkle with the dry seasonings mixture and bake for 6-7 minutes.

4. Let cool for a few minutes and enjoy.

NUTRITION:

Calories: 296; Fat: 22.7g; Protein: 22g; Carbohydrates: 1.8g.

MINTY ZUCCHINIS

PREPARATION TIME: 10 MINUTES | COOKING TIME: 15 MINUTES | SERVINGS: 4

INGREDIENTS:

1 pound zucchinis, sliced

1 tablespoon olive oil

2 garlic cloves, minced

1 tablespoon mint, chopped

pinch of salt and black pepper

¼ cup veggie stock

DIRECTIONS:

1. Heat up a pan with the oil over medium-high heat, add the garlic and sauté for 2 minutes.

2. Add the zucchinis and the other ingredients, toss, cook everything for 10 minutes more, divide between plates and serve.

NUTRITION:

Calories: 70; Fat: 1g; Protein: 6g; Carbohydrates: 0.5g.

CHEDDAR CAULIFLOWER BITES

PREPARATION TIME: 10 MINUTES | COOKING TIME: 25 MINUTES | SERVINGS: 8

INGREDIENTS:

1 pound cauliflower florets

1 teaspoon sweet paprika

A pinch of salt and black pepper

2 eggs, whisked

1 cup coconut flour

Cooking spray

1 cup cheddar cheese, grated

DIRECTIONS:

1. In a bowl, mix the flour with salt, pepper, cheese, and paprika and stir.

2. Put the eggs in a separate bowl.

3. Dredge the cauliflower florets in the eggs and then in the cheese mix, arrange them on a baking sheet lined with parchment paper and bake at 430°F for 25 minutes.

4. Serve as a snack.

NUTRITION:

Calories: 163; Fat: 12g; Protein: 7g; Carbohydrates: 2g.

MINI SALMON BITES

PREPARATION TIME: 10 MINUTES | COOKING TIME: 0 MINUTES | SERVINGS: 10

INGREDIENTS:

8 ounces cream cheese, softened

4 ounces salmon fillets, chopped

2 medium scallions, thinly sliced

Bagel seasoning, as required

DIRECTIONS:

1. In a bowl, add the cream cheese and beat until fluffy.
2. Add the salmon, and scallions and beat until well combined.
3. Make bite-sized balls from the mixture and lightly coat with the bagel seasoning.
4. Arrange the balls onto 2 parchment-lined baking sheets and refrigerate for about 2-3 hours before serving.
5. Enjoy!

NUTRITION:

Calories: 94; Fat: 8.4g; Protein: 3.8g; Carbohydrates: 0.8g.

DELIGHTFUL CAULIFLOWER POPPERS

PREPARATION TIME: 15 MINUTES | COOKING TIME: 30 MINUTES | SERVINGS: 4

INGREDIENTS:

4 cup cauliflower florets

2 teaspoon olive oil

¼ teaspoon chili powder

Salt and freshly ground black pepper, to taste

DIRECTIONS:

1. Preheat the oven to 450°F. Grease a roasting pan.
2. In a bowl, add all ingredients and toss to coat well.
3. Transfer the cauliflower mixture into a prepared roasting pan and spread in an even layer.
4. Roast for about 25-30 minutes.
5. Serve warm.

NUTRITION:

Calories: 46; Fat: 2.5g; Protein: 2g; Carbohydrates: 5.4g.

COCONUT CRAB CAKES

PREPARATION TIME: 20 MINUTES | COOKING TIME: 25 MINUTES | SERVINGS: 4

INGREDIENTS:

1 tablespoon minced garlic

2 pasteurized eggs

2 teaspoons coconut oil

¾ cup coconut flakes

¾ cup chopped spinach

¼ pound crabmeat

¼ cup chopped leek

½ cup extra virgin olive oil

½ teaspoon pepper

¼ onion diced

Salt

DIRECTIONS:

1. Pour the crabmeat in a bowl, then add in the coconut flakes and mix well.

2. Whisk eggs in a bowl, then mix in leek and spinach.

3. Season the egg mixture with pepper, two pinches of salt, and garlic.

4. Then, pour the eggs into the crab and stir well.

5. Preheat a pan, heat extra virgin olive, and fry the crab evenly from each side until golden brown. Remove from pan and serve hot.

NUTRITION:

Calories: 254; Fat: 9.5g; Protein: 8.9g; Carbohydrates: 4.1g.

BACON AND FETA SKEWERS

PREPARATION TIME: 15 MINUTES | COOKING TIME: 10 MINUTES | SERVINGS: 4

INGREDIENTS:

2 pounds feta cheese, cut into 8 cubes

8 bacon slices

4 bamboo skewers, soaked

1 zucchini, cut into 8 bite-size cubes

Salt and black pepper to taste

3 tablespoons avocado oil for brushing

DIRECTIONS:

1. Wrap each feta cube with a bacon slice.

2. Thread one wrapped feta on a skewer; add a zucchini cube, then another wrapped feta, and another zucchini.

3. Repeat the threading process with the remaining skewers.

4. Preheat a grill pan to medium heat, generously brush with the avocado oil and grill the skewer on both sides for 3 to 4 minutes per side or until the set is golden brown and the bacon cooked.

5. Serve and enjoy.

NUTRITION:

Calories: 290; Fat: 15.1g; Protein: 11.8g; Carbohydrates: 4.1g.

AVOCADO AND PROSCIUTTO DEVILED EGGS

PREPARATION TIME: 20 MINUTES | COOKING TIME: 10 MINUTES | SERVINGS: 4

INGREDIENTS:

4 eggs

Ice bath

4 prosciutto slices, chopped

1 avocado, pitted and peeled

1 tablespoon mustard

1 teaspoon plain vinegar

1 tablespoon heavy cream

1 tablespoon chopped fresh cilantro

Salt and black pepper to taste

½ cup mayonnaise

1 tablespoon coconut cream

¼ teaspoon cayenne pepper

1 tablespoon avocado oil

1 tablespoon chopped fresh parsley

DIRECTIONS:

1. Boil the eggs for 8 minutes.
2. Remove the eggs into the ice bath, sit for 3 minutes, and then peel the eggs.
3. Slice the eggs lengthwise into halves and empty the egg yolks into a bowl.
4. Arrange the egg whites on a plate with the whole side facing upwards.
5. While the eggs are cooking, heat a non-stick skillet over medium heat and cook the prosciutto for 5 to 8 minutes.
6. Remove the prosciutto onto a paper towel-lined plate to drain grease.
7. Put the avocado slices with the egg yolks and mash both ingredients with a fork until smooth.
8. Mix in the mustard, vinegar, heavy cream, cilantro, salt, and black pepper until well-blended.
9. Spoon the mixture into a piping bag and press the mixture into the egg holes until well-filled.
10. In a bowl, whisk the mayonnaise, coconut cream, cayenne pepper, and avocado oil.
11. On serving plates, spoon some of the mayonnaise sauce and slightly smear it in a circular movement. Top with the deviled eggs, scatter the prosciutto on top and garnish with the parsley.
12. Enjoy immediately.

NUTRITION:

Calories: 265; Fat: 11.7g; Protein: 7.9g; Carbohydrates: 3.1g.

DELECTABLE TOMATO SLICES

PREPARATION TIME: 15 MINUTES | COOKING TIME: 15 MINUTES | SERVINGS: 10

INGREDIENTS:

½ cup mayonnaise

½ cup ricotta cheese, shredded

½ cup part-skim mozzarella cheese, shredded

½ cup Parmesan and Romano cheese blend, grated

1 teaspoon garlic, minced

1 tablespoon dried oregano, crushed

Salt, to taste

4 large tomatoes, cut each one in 5 slices

DIRECTIONS:

1. Preheat the oven to broiler on high. Arrange a rack about 3-inch from the heating element.

2. In a bowl, add the mayonnaise, cheeses, garlic, oregano, and salt and mix until well combined and smooth.

3. Spread the cheese mixture over each tomato slice evenly.

4. Arrange the tomato slices onto a broiler pan in a single layer.

5. Broil for about 3-5 minutes or until the top becomes golden brown.

6. Remove from the oven and transfer the tomato slices onto a platter.

7. Set aside to cool slightly.

8. Serve warm.

NUTRITION:

Calories: 110; Fat: 57.4g; Protein: 5 g; Carbohydrates: 6.7g.

GRAIN-FREE TORTILLA CHIPS

PREPARATION TIME: 15 MINUTES | COOKING TIME: 16 MINUTES | SERVINGS: 6

INGREDIENTS:

1 ½ cups mozzarella cheese, shredded

½ cup almond flour

1 tablespoon golden flaxseed meal

Salt and freshly ground black pepper, to taste

DIRECTIONS:

1. Preheat the oven to 375°F. Line 2 large baking sheets with parchment paper.

2. In a microwave-safe bowl, add the cheese and microwave for about 1 minute, stirring after every 15 seconds.

3. In the bowl of melted cheese, add the almond flour, flaxseed meal, salt, and black pepper and with a fork, mix well.

4. With your hands, knead until a dough forms.

5. Make 2 equal sized balls from the dough.

6. Place 1 dough ball onto each prepared baking sheet and roll into an 8x10-inch rectangle.

7. Cut each dough rectangle into triangle-shaped chips.

8. Arrange the chips in a single layer.

9. Bake for about 10-15 minutes, flipping once halfway through.

10. Remove from oven and set aside to cool before serving.

NUTRITION:

Calories: 80; Fat: 6.3g; Protein: 4.2g; Carbohydrates: 2.6g.

CHEESES CHIPS

PREPARATION TIME: 15 MINUTES | COOKING TIME: 15 MINUTES | SERVINGS: 8

INGREDIENTS:

3 tablespoons coconut flour

½ cup strong cheddar cheese, grated and divided

¼ cup Parmesan cheese, grated

2 tablespoons butter, melted

1 organic egg

1 teaspoon fresh thyme leaves, minced

DIRECTIONS:

1. Preheat the oven to 350°F. Line a large baking sheet with parchment paper.

2. In a bowl, place the coconut flour, 1/4 cup of grated cheddar, Parmesan, butter, and egg and mix until well combined.

3. Set the mixture aside for about 3-5 minutes.

4. Make 8 equal-sized balls from the mixture.

5. Arrange the balls onto a prepared baking sheet in a single layer about 2-inch apart.

6. With your hands, press each ball into a little flat disc.

7. Sprinkle each disc with the remaining cheddar, followed by thyme.

8. Bake for about 13-15 minutes or until the edges become golden brown.

9. Remove from the oven and let them cool completely before serving.

NUTRITION:

Calories: 94; Fat: 7.1g; Protein: 4.2g; Carbohydrates: 3.2g.

SNACK PARTIES TREAT

PREPARATION TIME: 10 MINUTES | COOKING TIME: 6 MINUTES | SERVINGS: 4

INGREDIENTS:

8 bacon slices

8 mozzarella cheese sticks, frozen overnight

1 cup olive oil

DIRECTIONS:

1. Wrap a bacon slice around each cheese stick and secure with a toothpick.

2. In a cast-iron skillet, heat the oil over medium heat and fry the mozzarella sticks in 2 batches for about 2-3 minutes or until golden brown from all sides.

3. With a slotted spoon, transfer the mozzarella sticks onto a paper towel-lined plate to drain.

4. Set aside to cool slightly.

5. Serve warm.

NUTRITION:

Calories: 798; Fat: 76.3g; Protein: 30.1g; Carbohydrates: 2.5g.

POULTRY RECIPES

DELICIOUS CHICKEN WINGS

PREPARATION TIME: 10 MINUTES | COOKING TIME: 30 MINUTES | SERVINGS: 6

INGREDIENTS:

1 egg, beaten

1 ½ pounds chicken wings, skinless

6 tablespoons olive oil

½ cup apple cider vinegar

½ teaspoon cayenne pepper

2 garlic cloves, minced

½ teaspoon pepper

¾ teaspoon salt

DIRECTIONS:

1. Add all ingredients except chicken in a large bowl and mix well.
2. Add chicken wings in a bowl and mix until well coated and set aside for 20 minutes.
3. Preheat the oven to 450°F.
4. Spray a baking tray with cooking spray.
5. Place marinated wings on a prepared baking tray and bake for 30 minutes.
6. Serve and enjoy.

NUTRITION:

Calories: 355; Fat: 23g; Protein: 33g; Carbohydrates: 0.5g.

LEMON CHICKEN

PREPARATION TIME: 10 MINUTES | COOKING TIME: 45 MINUTES | SERVINGS: 8

INGREDIENTS:

8 chicken breasts, skinless and boneless

¼ cup fresh lemon juice

2 tablespoons green onion, chopped

1 tablespoon oregano leaves

3 ounces feta cheese, crumbled

¼ teaspoon pepper

DIRECTIONS:

1. Preheat the oven to 350°F.
2. Spray baking dish with cooking spray.
3. Place chicken breasts in prepared baking dish.
4. Drizzle with 2 tablespoons lemon juice and sprinkle with 1/2 tablespoon oregano and pepper.
5. Top with green onion and crumbled cheese.
6. Drizzle with remaining lemon juice and oregano.
7. Bake for 45 minutes.
8. Serve and enjoy.

NUTRITION:

Calories: 246; Fat: 10.8g; Protein: 34g; Carbohydrates: 1.2g.

TASTY SHREDDED CHICKEN

PREPARATION TIME: 10 MINUTES | COOKING TIME: 25 MINUTES | SERVINGS: 6

INGREDIENTS:

3 chicken breasts, boneless and skinless

¼ cup vinegar

13.5 ounces chunky salsa

¼ teaspoon onion powder

1 tablespoon ground cumin

1 ½ tablespoons chili powder

DIRECTIONS:

1. Add all ingredients into the instant pot and stir well.

2. Seal pot with lid and cook on manual high pressure for 25 minutes.

3. Once done, release the pressure using the quick-release method, then open the lid.

4. Remove chicken from pot and shred using a fork.

5. Serve and enjoy.

NUTRITION:

Calories: 171; Fat: 6.3g; Protein: 23g; Carbohydrates: 5g.

CHICKEN BACON SALAD

PREPARATION TIME: 10 MINUTES | COOKING TIME: 10 MINUTES | SERVINGS: 4

INGREDIENTS:

2 chicken breasts, cooked and chopped

3 bacon slices, cooked and chopped

½ cup celery, diced

2 avocado, chopped

2 ½ tablespoons olive oil

3 tablespoons fresh lemon juice

½ teaspoon dried dill

1 tablespoon dried chives

½ teaspoon pepper

1 teaspoon salt

DIRECTIONS:

1. Add all ingredients into the large bowl and toss well to combine.

2. Serve and enjoy.

NUTRITION:

Calories: 441; Fat: 36g; Protein: 24g; Carbohydrates: 10g.

FLAVORFUL HERB CHICKEN

PREPARATION TIME: 10 MINUTES | COOKING TIME: 15 MINUTES | SERVINGS: 5

INGREDIENTS:

2 pounds chicken breast, skinless and boneless

½ cup Greek yogurt

¼ cup mayonnaise

1 ½ teaspoons herb seasoning

½ teaspoon onion powder

½ teaspoon garlic powder

¼ teaspoon salt

DIRECTIONS:

1. Preheat the air-fryer to 380°F.
2. In a small bowl, mix together mayonnaise, herb seasoning, onion powder, garlic powder, and yogurt.
3. Coat chicken with mayo mixture.
4. Spray air-fryer basket with cooking spray.
5. Place chicken in an air-fryer basket and cook for 15 minutes. Turn halfway through.
6. Serve and enjoy.

NUTRITION:

Calories: 272; Fat: 8g; Protein: 40g; Carbohydrates: 5g.

CARIBBEAN-STYLE CHICKEN WINGS

PREPARATION TIME: 10 MINUTES | COOKING TIME: 50 MINUTES | SERVINGS: 2

INGREDIENTS:

4 chicken wings, skinless

1 tablespoon coconut aminos

2 tablespoons rum

2 tablespoons butter

1 tablespoon onion powder

1 tablespoon garlic powder

½ teaspoon salt

¼ teaspoon freshly ground black pepper

½ teaspoon red pepper flakes

¼ teaspoon dried dill

2 tablespoons sesame seeds

DIRECTIONS:

1. Pat dry the chicken wings. Toss the chicken wings with the remaining ingredients until well coated. Arrange the chicken wings on a parchment-lined baking sheet.

2. Bake in the preheated oven at 430°F for 45 minutes until golden brown.

3. Serve with your favorite sauce for dipping. Bon appétit!

NUTRITION:

Calories: 225; Fat: 18.5g; Protein: 15.6g; Carbohydrates: 5.2g.

MEAT RECIPES

COFFEE BUTTER RUBBED TRI-TIP STEAK

PREPARATION TIME: 20 MINUTES | COOKING TIME: 15 MINUTES | SERVINGS: 2

INGREDIENTS:

2 Tri-tip steaks, preferably ½ pound

1 package of coffee blocks

½ tablespoon garlic powder

1 teaspoon black pepper, coarse ground

2 tablespoons olive oil

½ tablespoon sea salt

DIRECTIONS:

1. Pound the meat using a mallet until tenderize; let the meat sit for 20 minutes at room temperature.

2. Combine everything together (except the steaks) in a large-sized mixing bowl.

3. Rub the sides, top, and bottom of the meat steaks entirely with the mixture.

4. Over medium-high heat in a large skillet; heat the olive oil until hot.

5. Carefully add the coated steaks into the hot oil and cook for 5 minutes.

6. Flip and cook the other side until cooked through, for 5 more minutes.

7. Remove the meat from the pan and let sit for a minute in its own juices.

8. Cut into slices against the grain. Serve warm and enjoy.

NUTRITION:

Calories: 371; Fat: 35g; Protein: 22g; Carbohydrates: 0.5g.

KETO RIB EYE STEAK

PREPARATION TIME: 5 MINUTES | COOKING TIME: 20 MINUTES | SERVINGS: 2

INGREDIENTS:

½ pound grass-fed rib-eye steak, preferably 1" thick

1 teaspoon Adobo Seasoning

1 tablespoon extra-virgin olive oil

Pepper and sea salt to taste

DIRECTIONS:

1. Add steak in a large-sized mixing bowl and drizzle both sides with a small amount of olive oil.
2. Dust the seasonings on both sides; rubbing the seasonings into the meat.
3. Let sit for a couple of minutes and heat up your grill in advance.
4. Once hot; place the steaks over the grill, and cook until both sides are cooked through, for 15 to 20 minutes, flipping occasionally.

NUTRITION:

Calories: 257; Fat: 19g; Protein: 24g; Carbohydrates: 0.3g.

SPICY BEEF MEATBALLS

PREPARATION TIME: 10 MINUTES | COOKING TIME: 10 MINUTES | SERVINGS: 3

INGREDIENTS:

1 cup mozzarella or cheddar cheese; cut into cubes

1 pound minced ground beef

1 teaspoon olive oil

3 tablespoons parmesan cheese

1 teaspoon garlic powder

½ teaspoon each of pepper, and salt

DIRECTIONS:

1. Thoroughly combine the ground beef with the entire dry ingredients; mix well.
2. Wrap the cheese cubes into the mince; forming 9 meatballs from the prepared mixture.
3. Pan-fry the formed meatballs until cooked through, covered (uncover and stirring frequently).

NUTRITION:

Calories: 595; Fat: 44g; Protein: 49g; Carbohydrates: 2.8g.

TURKEY AND RADISHES

PREPARATION TIME: 5 MINUTES | COOKING TIME: 12 MINUTES | SERVINGS: 4

INGREDIENTS:

1 tablespoon olive oil

1 pound radishes, trimmed and quartered

1 pound cooked turkey, chopped

1 onion, small, chopped

½ cup beef broth

Pepper and salt to taste

DIRECTIONS:

1. Over medium high heat settings in a large saucepan, heat a tablespoon of olive oil.

2. Once hot, add and sauté the onion for a couple of minutes and then add the radishes; continue to sauté for 5 more minutes.

3. Add in the beef broth; give everything a good stir until evenly mixed. Cover the pan loosely and cook until the liquid is reduced and the radishes are fork-tender for 5 minutes.

4. Add in the cooked turkey. Season with pepper and salt to taste, giving everything a good stir. Serve immediately and enjoy.

NUTRITION:

Calories: 304; Fat: 16g; Protein: 31g; Carbohydrates: 6.5g.

SPICY STEAK CURRY

PREPARATION TIME: 15 MINUTES | COOKING TIME: 40 MINUTES | SERVINGS: 6

INGREDIENTS:

1 cup plain yogurt

½ teaspoon garlic paste

½ teaspoon ginger paste

½ teaspoon ground cloves

½ teaspoon ground cumin

2 teaspoons red pepper flakes

¼ teaspoon ground turmeric

Salt

2 pounds grass-fed round steak

¼ cup olive oil

1 medium yellow onion

1 ½ tablespoons lemon juice

¼ cup cilantro

DIRECTIONS:

1. Mix yogurt, garlic paste, ginger paste, and spices. Add the steak pieces. Set aside.
2. Sauté the onion for 4-5 minutes. Add the steak pieces with the marinade and mix.
3. Simmer for 25 minutes. Stir in the lemon juice and simmer 10 minutes.
4. Garnish with cilantro and serve.

NUTRITION:

Calories: 440; Fat: 19g; Protein: 48.3g; Carbohydrates: 5.5g.

BEEF STEW

PREPARATION TIME: 15 MINUTES | COOKING TIME: 1 HOUR 40 MINUTES | SERVINGS: 4

INGREDIENTS:

1 1/3 pounds grass-fed chuck roast

Salt

Ground black pepper

2 tablespoons butter

1 yellow onion

2 garlic cloves

1 cup beef broth

1 bay leaf

½ teaspoon dried thyme

½ teaspoon dried rosemary

1 carrot

4 ounces celery stalks

1 tablespoon lemon juice

DIRECTIONS:

1. Put salt and black pepper in beef cubes.
2. Sear the beef cubes for 4-5 minutes. Add the onion and garlic, then adjust the heat to medium and cook for 4-5 minutes. Add the broth, bay leaf, and dried herbs and boil.
3. Simmer for 45 minutes. Stir in the carrot and celery and simmer for 30-45 minutes.
4. Stir in lemon juice, salt, and black pepper. Serve.

NUTRITION:

Calories: 413; Fat: 16g; Protein: 52g; Carbohydrates: 5.9g.

BEEF & CABBAGE STEW

PREPARATION TIME: 15 MINUTES | COOKING TIME: 2 HOURS 10 MINUTES | SERVINGS: 8

INGREDIENTS:

2 pounds grass-fed beef stew meat

1 1/3 cups hot chicken broth

2 yellow onions

2 bay leaves

1 teaspoon Greek seasoning

Salt

Ground black pepper

3 celery stalks

1 package cabbage

1 can sugar-free tomato sauce

1 can sugar-free whole plum tomatoes

DIRECTIONS:

1. Sear the beef for 4-5 minutes. Stir in the broth, onion, bay leaves, Greek seasoning, salt, and black pepper and boil. Adjust the heat to low and cook for 1¼ hours.

2. Stir in the celery and cabbage and cook for 30 minutes. Stir in the tomato sauce and chopped plum tomatoes and cook, uncovered for 15-20 minutes. Stir in the salt, discard bay leaves and serve.

NUTRITION:

Calories: 247; Fat: 16g; Protein: 36.5g; Carbohydrates: 7g.

STEAK WITH BLUEBERRY SAUCE

PREPARATION TIME: 15 MINUTES | COOKING TIME: 20 MINUTES | SERVINGS: 4

INGREDIENTS:

For sauce:

2 tablespoons butter

2 tablespoons yellow onion

2 garlic cloves

1 teaspoon thyme

1 1/3 cups beef broth

2 tablespoons lemon juice

¾ cup blueberries

For steak:

2 tablespoons butter

4 grass-fed flank steaks

Salt

Ground black pepper

DIRECTIONS:

1. For the sauce: sauté the onion for 2-3 minutes.
2. Add the garlic and thyme and sauté for 1 minute. Stir in the broth and simmer for 10 minutes.
3. For the steak: put salt and black pepper. Cook steaks for 3-4 minutes per side.
4. Transfer and put aside. Add sauce in the skillet and stir. Stir in the lemon juice, blueberries, salt, and black pepper and cook for 1-2 minutes. Put blueberry sauce over the steaks. Serve.

NUTRITION:

Calories. 407; Fat: 19.7g; Protein; 49.5g; Carbohydrates: 5.7g

BEEF TACO BAKE

PREPARATION TIME: 15 MINUTES | COOKING TIME: 1 HOUR | SERVINGS: 6

INGREDIENTS:

For crust:

3 organic eggs

4 ounces cream cheese

½ teaspoon taco seasoning

1/3 cup heavy cream

8 ounces cheddar cheese

For topping:

1 pound grass-fed ground beef

4 ounces green chilies

¼ cup sugar-free tomato sauce

3 teaspoons taco seasoning

8 ounces cheddar cheese

DIRECTIONS:

1. Warm-up oven to 375°F.
2. For the crust: beat the eggs, and cream cheese, taco seasoning, and heavy cream.
3. Place cheddar cheese in the baking dish. Spread cream cheese mixture over cheese.
4. Bake for 25-30 minutes. Remove, then set aside for 5 minutes.
5. For topping: Cook the beef for 8-10 minutes.
6. Stir in the green chilies, tomato sauce, and taco seasoning and transfer.
7. Place the beef mixture over the crust and sprinkle with cheese. Bake for 18-20 minutes.
8. Remove, then slice and serve.

NUTRITION:

Calories: 569; Fat: g; Protein: 38.7g; Carbohydrates: 4g.

MEATBALLS IN CHEESE SAUCE

PREPARATION TIME: 20 MINUTES | COOKING TIME: 25 MINUTES | SERVINGS: 5

INGREDIENTS:

For meatballs:

1 pound ground pork

1 organic egg

2 ounces Parmesan cheese

½ tablespoon dried basil

1 teaspoon garlic powder

½ teaspoon onion powder

Salt

Ground black pepper

3 tablespoons olive oil

For sauce:

1 can sugar-free tomatoes

2 tablespoons butter

7 ounces spinach

2 tablespoons parsley

5 ounces mozzarella cheese

Salt

Ground black pepper

DIRECTIONS:

1. For meatballs: Mix all the ingredients for the meatballs, except oil in a large bowl. Make small-sized balls from the mixture.

2. Cook the meatballs for 3-5 minutes. Add the tomatoes. Simmer for 15 minutes.

3. Stir fry the spinach for 1-2 minutes in butter. Add salt and black pepper.

4. Remove, then put the cooked spinach, parsley, and mozzarella cheese into meatballs and stir.

5. Cook for 1-2 minutes. Remove and serve.

NUTRITION:

Calories: 398; Fat: 24.8g; Protein: 38.6g; Carbohydrates: 6.6g.

CHOCOLATE CHILI

PREPARATION TIME: 15 MINUTES | COOKING TIME: 2 HOURS AND 15 MINUTES | SERVINGS: 8

INGREDIENTS:

2 tablespoons olive oil

1 small onion

1 green bell pepper

4 garlic cloves

1 jalapeño pepper

1 teaspoon dried thyme

2 tablespoons red chili powder

1 tablespoon ground cumin

2 pounds lean ground pork

2 cups fresh tomatoes

4 ounces sugar-free tomato paste

1 ½ tablespoons cacao powder

2 cups chicken broth

1 cup water

Salt

Ground black pepper

¼ cup cheddar cheese

DIRECTIONS:

1. Sauté the onion and bell pepper for 5-7 minutes.

2. Add the garlic, jalapeño pepper, thyme, and spices and sauté for 1 minute.

3. Add the pork and cook for 4-5 minutes. Stir in the tomatoes, tomato paste, and cacao powder and cook for 2 minutes.

4. Add the broth and water, boil. Simmer, covered for 2 hours. Stir in the salt and black pepper. Remove, then top with cheddar cheese and serve.

NUTRITION:

Calories: 326; Fat: 22.9g; Protein: 23.3g; Carbohydrates: 9.1g.

PORK STEW

PREPARATION TIME: 15 MINUTES | COOKING TIME: 45 MINUTES | SERVINGS: 6

INGREDIENTS:

2 tablespoons olive oil

2 pounds pork tenderloin

1 tablespoon garlic

2 teaspoons paprika

¾ cup chicken broth

1 cup sugar-free tomato sauce

½ tablespoon Erythritol

1 teaspoon dried oregano

2 dried bay leaves

2 tablespoons lemon juice

Salt

Ground black pepper

DIRECTIONS:

1. Cook the pork for 3-4 minutes. Add the garlic and cook for 1 minute.

2. Stir in the remaining fixing and boil. Simmer, covered for 30-40 minutes

3. Remove, then discard the bay leaves. Serve.

NUTRITION:

Calories: 277; Fat: 10.4g; Protein: 41g; Carbohydrates: 3.6g.

PORK & CHILIES STEW

PREPARATION TIME: 15 MINUTES | COOKING TIME: 2 HOURS AND 10 MINUTES | SERVINGS: 8

INGREDIENTS:

3 tablespoons unsalted butter

2 ½ pounds boneless pork ribs

1 large yellow onion

4 garlic cloves

1 ½ cups chicken broth

2 cans sugar-free tomatoes

1 cup canned roasted poblano chilies

2 teaspoons dried oregano

1 teaspoon ground cumin

Salt

¼ cup cilantro

2 tablespoons lime juice

DIRECTIONS:

1. Cook the pork, onions, and garlic for 5 minutes.

2. Add the broth, tomatoes, poblano chilies, oregano, cumin, and salt and boil.

3. Simmer, covered for 2 hours. Mix with the fresh cilantro and lime juice and remove it. Serve.

NUTRITION:

Calories: 288; Fat: 13.6g; Protein: 39.6g; Carbohydrates: 8.8g.

SEAFOOD AND FISH RECIPES

HERBED SEA BASS

PREPARATION TIME: 15 MINUTES | COOKING TIME: 20 MINUTES | SERVINGS: 2

INGREDIENTS:

2 (1¼-pound) whole sea bass; gutted, gilled, scaled, and fins removed

Salt and ground black pepper, to taste

6 fresh bay leaves

2 fresh thyme sprigs

2 fresh parsley sprigs

2 fresh rosemary sprigs

2 tablespoons butter, melted

2 tablespoons fresh lemon juice

DIRECTIONS:

1. Season the cavity and outer side of each fish with salt and black pepper evenly.

2. With plastic wrap, cover each fish and refrigerate for 1 hour.

3. Preheat the oven to 450°F.

4. Lightly grease a baking dish.

5. Arrange 2 bay leaves in the bottom of the prepared baking dish.

6. Divide herb sprigs and remaining bay leaves inside the cavity of each fish.

7. Arrange both fish over bay leaves in baking dish and drizzle with butter.

8. Roast for about 15–20 minutes or until fish is cooked through.

9. Remove the baking dish from the oven and place the fish onto a platter.

10. Drizzle the fish with lemon juice and serve.

NUTRITION:

Calories: 192; Fat: 6g; Protein: 29g; Carbohydrates. 4.2g.

SUPER SALMON PARCEL

PREPARATION TIME: 15 MINUTES | COOKING TIME: 20 MINUTES | SERVINGS: 6

INGREDIENTS:

6 (3-ounce) salmon fillets

Salt and freshly ground black pepper, to taste

1 yellow bell pepper, seeded and cubed

1 red bell pepper, seeded and cubed

4 plum tomatoes, cubed

1 small yellow onion, sliced thinly

½ cup fresh parsley, chopped

¼ cup olive oil

2 tablespoons fresh lemon juice

DIRECTIONS:

1. Preheat the oven to 400°F.

2. Arrange 6 pieces of foil onto a smooth surface. Place 1 salmon fillet onto each foil piece and sprinkle with salt and black pepper. In a bowl, add the bell peppers, tomato and onion and mix. Place veggie mixture over each fillet evenly and top with parsley. Drizzle with oil and lemon juice. Fold the foil around salmon mixture to seal it. Arrange the foil packets onto a large baking sheet in a single layer. Bake for about 20 minutes.

3. Serve hot.

NUTRITION:

Calories: 224; Fat: 14g; Protein: 18.2g; Carbohydrates: 8.2g.

JUICY GARLIC BUTTER SHRIMP

PREPARATION TIME: 10 MINUTES | COOKING TIME: 5 MINUTES | SERVINGS: 4

INGREDIENTS:

2 pounds shrimp, peeled and deveined

2 tablespoons fresh herbs, chopped

2 tablespoons fresh lemon juice

1 teaspoon paprika

1 tablespoon garlic, minced

¼ cup butter

Pepper

Salt

DIRECTIONS:

1. Melt butter in a pan over medium heat.
2. Add garlic and sauté for 30 seconds.
3. Add shrimp, paprika, pepper, and salt. Cook shrimp for 2 minutes on each side.
4. Add remaining ingredients, stir well and cook for 1 minute.
5. Serve and enjoy.

NUTRITION:

Calories: 379; Fat: 15.5g; Protein: 52.1g; Carbohydrates: 5g.

EASY BAKED SHRIMP SCAMPI

PREPARATION TIME: 10 MINUTES | COOKING TIME: 10 MINUTES | SERVINGS: 4

INGREDIENTS:

2 pounds shrimp, peeled

¾ cup olive oil

2 teaspoons dried oregano

1 tablespoon garlic, minced

½ cup fresh lemon juice

¼ cup butter, sliced

Pepper

Salt

DIRECTIONS:

1. Preheat the oven to 350°F. Add shrimp in a baking dish. In a bowl, whisk together lemon juice, oregano, garlic, oil, pepper, and salt and pour over shrimp. Add butter on top of shrimp.
2. Bake in preheated oven for 10 minutes or until shrimp cooked. Serve and enjoy.

NUTRITION:

Calories: 708; Fat: 53.5g; Protein: 52.2g; Carbohydrates: 5.3g.

FLAVORFUL SHRIMP CREOLE

PREPARATION TIME: 10 MINUTES | COOKING TIME: 1 HOUR 30 MINUTES | SERVINGS: 8

INGREDIENTS:

2 pounds shrimp, peeled

¾ cup green onions, chopped

1 teaspoon garlic, minced

2 ½ cups water

1 tablespoon hot sauce

8 ounces can tomato sauce, sugar-free

8 ounces can tomato paste

½ cup bell pepper, chopped

¾ cup celery, chopped

1 cup onion, chopped

2 tablespoons olive oil

Pepper

Salt

DIRECTIONS:

1. Heat oil in a saucepan over medium heat.

2. Add celery, onion, bell pepper, pepper, and salt and sauté until onion is softened.

3. Add tomato paste and cook for 5 minutes.

4. Add hot sauce, tomato sauce, and water and cook for 1 hour.

5. Add garlic and shrimp and cook for 15 minutes.

6. Add green onions and cook for 2 minutes more.

7. Serve and enjoy.

NUTRITION:

Calories: 208; Fat: 5.7g; Protein: 27.92g; Carbohydrates: 11.6g.

DELICIOUS BLACKENED SHRIMP

PREPARATION TIME: 10 MINUTES | COOKING TIME: 5 MINUTES | SERVINGS: 4

INGREDIENTS:

1 ½ pounds shrimp, peeled

1 tablespoon garlic, minced

1 tablespoon olive oil

1 teaspoon garlic powder

1 teaspoon dried oregano

1 teaspoon cumin

1 tablespoon paprika

1 tablespoon chili powder

Pepper

Salt

DIRECTIONS:

1. In a mixing bowl, mix together garlic powder, oregano, cumin, paprika, chili powder, pepper, and salt.
2. Add shrimp and mix until well-coated. Set aside for 30 minutes.
3. Heat oil in a pan over medium-high heat.
4. Add shrimp and cook for 2 minutes. Turn shrimp and cook for 2 minutes more.
5. Add garlic and cook for 30 seconds.
6. Serve and enjoy.

NUTRITION:

Calories: 252; Fat: 7.1g; Protein: 39.6g; Carbohydrates: 6.3g.

SIMPLE LEMON GARLIC SHRIMP

PREPARATION TIME: 5 MINUTES | COOKING TIME: 15 MINUTES | SERVINGS: 4

INGREDIENTS:

1 ½ pounds shrimp, peeled and deveined

¼ cup fresh parsley, chopped

¼ cup fresh lemon juice

1 tablespoon garlic, minced

¼ cup butter

Pepper

Salt

DIRECTIONS:

1. Melt butter in a pan over medium heat. Add garlic and sauté for 30 seconds.
2. Add shrimp and season with pepper and salt and cook for 4-5 minutes or until it turns to pink.
3. Add lemon juice and parsley, stir well and cook for 2 minutes. Serve and enjoy.

NUTRITION:

Calories: 312; Fat: 14.6g; Protein: 39.2g; Carbohydrates: 3.9g.

PERFECT PAN-SEARED SCALLOPS

PREPARATION TIME: 10 MINUTES | COOKING TIME: 4 MINUTES | SERVINGS: 4

INGREDIENTS:

1 pound scallops, rinse and pat dry

1 tablespoon olive oil

2 tablespoons butter

Pepper

Salt

DIRECTIONS:

1. Season scallops with pepper and salt.
2. Heat butter and oil in a pan over medium heat.
3. Add scallops and sear for 2 minutes, then turn to other side and cook for 2 minutes more.
4. Serve and enjoy.

NUTRITION:

Calories: 181; Fat: 10.1g; Protein: 19.1g; Carbohydrates: 2.7g.

SALAD RECIPES

BACON AVOCADO SALAD

PREPARATION TIME: 20 MINUTES | COOKING TIME: 0 MINUTES | SERVINGS: 4

INGREDIENTS:

2 hard-boiled eggs, chopped

2 cups spinach

2 large avocados, 1 chopped and 1 sliced

2 small lettuce heads, chopped

1 spring onion, sliced

4 cooked bacon slices, crumbled

For the vinaigrette:

Olive oil

Mustard

Apple cider vinegar

DIRECTIONS:

1. In a large bowl, mix the eggs, spinach, avocados, lettuce, and onion. Set aside.

2. Make the vinaigrette: In a separate bowl, add the olive oil, mustard, and apple cider vinegar. Mix well.

3. Pour the vinaigrette into the large bowl and toss well.

4. Serve topped with bacon slices and sliced avocado.

NUTRITION:

Calories: 268; Fat: 16.9g; Protein: 5g; Carbohydrates: 8g.

CAULIFLOWER, SHRIMP, AND CUCUMBER SALAD

PREPARATION TIME: 10 MINUTES | COOKING TIME: 15 MINUTES | SERVINGS: 6

INGREDIENTS:

¼ cup olive oil

1 pound (454 g) medium shrimp

1 cauliflower head, florets only

2 cucumbers, peeled and chopped

For the dressing:

Olive oil

Lemon juice

Lemon zest

Dill

Salt and pepper

DIRECTIONS:

1. In a skillet over medium heat, heat the olive oil until sizzling hot. Add the shrimp and cook for 8 minutes, stirring occasionally, or until the flesh is pink and opaque.

2. Meanwhile, in a microwave-safe bowl, add the cauliflower florets and microwave for about 5 minutes until tender.

3. Remove the shrimp from the heat to a large bowl. Add the cauliflower and cucumber to the shrimp in the bowl. Set aside.

4. Make the dressing: Mix the olive oil, lemon juice, lemon zest, dill, salt, and pepper in a third bowl. Pour the dressing into the bowl of shrimp mixture. Toss well until the shrimp and vegetables are coated thoroughly.

5. Serve immediately or refrigerate for 1 hour before serving.

NUTRITION:

Calories: 308; Fat: 19g; Protein: 5g; Carbohydrates: 4g.

BACON BLEU ZOODLE SALAD

PREPARATION TIME: 5 MINUTES | COOKING TIME: 0 MINUTES | SERVINGS: 2

INGREDIENTS:

4 cups zucchini noodles

½ cup bacon, cooked and crumbled

1 cup fresh spinach, chopped

1/3 cup bleu cheese, crumbled

Fresh cracked pepper, to taste

DIRECTIONS:

1. Toss the entire ingredients together in a large-sized mixing bowl. Serve immediately, and enjoy.

NUTRITION:

Calories: 214; Fat: 17g; Protein: 33g; Carbohydrates: 6g.

SALMON AND LETTUCE SALAD

PREPARATION TIME: 10 MINUTES | COOKING TIME: 0 MINUTES | SERVINGS: 4

INGREDIENTS:

1 tablespoon extra-virgin olive oil

2 salmon fillets, chopped

3 tablespoons mayonnaise

1 tablespoon lime juice

Sea salt, to taste

1 cup romaine lettuce, shredded

1 teaspoon onion flakes

½ avocado, sliced

DIRECTIONS:

1. In a bowl, stir together the olive oil, salmon, mayo, lime juice, and salt. Stir well until the salmon is coated fully.

2. Divide evenly the romaine lettuce and onion flakes among four serving plates. Spread the salmon mixture over the lettuce, then serve topped with avocado slices.

NUTRITION:

Calories: 271; Fat: 18g; Protein: 6g; Carbohydrates: 4g.

SHRIMP, TOMATO, AND AVOCADO SALAD

PREPARATION TIME: 5 MINUTES | COOKING TIME: 0 MINUTES | SERVINGS: 4

INGREDIENTS:

1 pound (454 g) shrimp, shelled and deveined

2 tomatoes, cubed

2 avocados, peeled and cubed

A handful of fresh cilantro, chopped

4 green onions, minced

Juice of 1 lime or lemon

1 tablespoon macadamia nut or avocado oil

Celtic sea salt and fresh ground black pepper, to taste

DIRECTIONS:

1. Combine the shrimp, tomatoes, avocados, cilantro, and onions in a large bowl.

2. Squeeze the lemon juice over the vegetables in the large bowl, then drizzle with avocado oil and sprinkle the salt and black pepper to season. Toss to combine well.

3. You can cover the salad, and refrigerate to chill for 45 minutes or serve immediately.

NUTRITION:

Calories: 158; Fat: 10g; Protein: 9g; Carbohydrates: 4g.

CHILI-LIME TUNA SALAD

PREPARATION TIME: 10 MINUTES | COOKING TIME: 0 MINUTES | SERVINGS: 2

INGREDIENTS:

1 tablespoon lime juice

1/3 cup mayonnaise

¼ teaspoon salt

1 teaspoon Tajin chili lime seasoning

1/8 teaspoon pepper

1 medium stalk celery (finely chopped)

2 cups romaine lettuce (chopped roughly)

2 tablespoons red onion (finely chopped)

Optional: chopped green onion, black pepper, lemon juice

5 ounces canned tuna

DIRECTIONS:

1. Using a bowl of medium size, mix some of the ingredients, such as lime, pepper, and chili-lime.

2. Then, add tuna and vegetables to the pot and stir. Enjoy!

NUTRITION:

Calories: 259; Fat: 11.3g; Protein: 12.9g; Carbohydrates: 2.9g.

PESTO CHICKEN SALAD

PREPARATION TIME: 4 MINUTES | COOKING TIME: 20 MINUTES | SERVINGS: 4

INGREDIENTS:

4 pieces chicken breast

½ cup of pesto

1 cup cherry tomatoes

3 cups spinach

A dash of salt

3 tablespoons olive oil

DIRECTIONS:

1. For another alternative for plain old, baked chicken, you will want to consider this delicious Pesto chicken salad! To start, prep the stove to 350°F. As this warms up, place your chicken pieces onto a baking plate and coat with the pepper, salt, and olive oil. When this is done, pop the dish into the oven for 40 minutes.

2. When the chicken is cooked through and no longer pink on the inside, take it out of the oven and cool slightly before handling.

3. Once you can handle the chicken, toss it into a bowl along with the pesto and your sliced tomatoes. When the ingredients are mixed to your liking, place over a bowl of fresh spinach and enjoy your salad.

NUTRITION:

Calories: 188; Fat: 19g; Protein: 20g; Carbohydrates: 5g.

VEGETABLE RECIPES

CAULIFLOWER RICE

PREPARATION TIME: 20 MINUTES | COOKING TIME: 8 MINUTES | SERVINGS: 2

INGREDIENTS:

1 head of cauliflower

1 tablespoon of olive oil or grass-fed butter

Salt to taste

DIRECTIONS:

1. Slice the cauliflower into small pieces with a sharp knife, add in a food processor, and process it until fully broken.
2. If any pieces are left unprocessed, put them back in and process them again.
3. Preheat a large pan and heat olive oil in it.
4. Add in your processed cauliflower with a pinch of salt.
5. Cover and cook for 4-8 minutes.
6. Then, serve warm.

NUTRITION:

Calories: 204; Fat: 11g; Protein: 1.5g; Carbohydrates: 4.2g.

ROASTED OKRA

PREPARATION TIME: 3 MINUTES | COOKING TIME: 6 MINUTES | SERVINGS: 4

INGREDIENTS:

½ pound sliced okra

1 teaspoon olive oil

Salt and black pepper, to taste

DIRECTIONS:

1. Preheat the air fryer at 350°F for 5 min.

2. Season okra with olive oil, pepper, and salt.

3. Air fry for minutes, toss, and again air fry for 3 minutes. Relish.

NUTRITION:

Calories: 112; Fat: 5g; Protein: 4.7g; Carbohydrates:16g.

PARMESAN ZUCCHINI FRIES

PREPARATION TIME: 5 MINUTES | COOKING TIME: 20 MINUTES | SERVINGS: 2

INGREDIENTS:

1 thinly sliced Zucchini

1 large beaten egg

¾ cup crated Parmesan cheese

1 cup panko bread crumbs

DIRECTIONS:

1. First, preheat the air fryer at 350°F.

2. Mix panko bread crumbs and parmesan cheese. Dip zucchini in egg and then coat with panko bread crumbs mixture. Gently press to firm the coating.

3. Air fry the zucchini fries for 10 minutes, shake the air fryer basket, and again air fry for 5 minutes.

4. Serve with coleslaw. Relish.

NUTRITION:

Calories: 160; Fat: 6.5g; Protein: 10.9g; Carbohydrates: 21g.

CREAMY ZOODLES

PREPARATION TIME: 15 MINUTES | COOKING TIME: 10 MINUTES | SERVINGS: 4

INGREDIENTS:

1 cup heavy whipping cream

1/4 cup mayonnaise

Salt and ground black pepper, as required

30 ounces zucchini, spiralized with blade C

3 ounces Parmesan cheese, grated

2 tablespoons fresh mint leaves

2 tablespoons butter, melted

DIRECTIONS:

1. The heavy cream must be added to a pan then bring to a boil.
2. Lower the heat to low and cook until reduced in half.
3. Put in the pepper, mayo, and salt; cook until the mixture is warm enough.
4. Add the zucchini noodles and gently stir to combine.
5. Stir in the Parmesan cheese.
6. Divide the zucchini noodles onto four serving plates and immediately drizzle with the melted butter.
7. Serve immediately.

NUTRITION:

Calories: 241; Fat: 11.4g; Protein: 5.1g; Carbohydrates: 3.1g.

BAKED ZUCCHINI GRATIN

PREPARATION TIME: 25 MINUTES | COOKING TIME: 25 MINUTES | SERVINGS: 2

INGREDIENTS:

1 large zucchini, cut into 1/4-inch-thick slices

1 ounce Brie cheese, rind trimmed off

1 tablespoon butter

Freshly ground black pepper

1/3 cup shredded Gruyere cheese

1/4 cup crushed pork rinds

DIRECTIONS:

1. Preheat the oven to 400°F.

2. When the zucchini has been "weeping" for about 30 minutes, in a small saucepan over medium-low heat, heat the Brie and butter, occasionally stirring, until the cheese has melted.

3. The mixture is thoroughly combined for about 2 minutes.

4. Arrange the zucchini in an 8-inch baking dish, so the zucchini slices are overlapping a bit.

5. Season with pepper.

6. Pour the Brie mixture over the zucchini, and top with the shredded Gruyere cheese.

7. Sprinkle the crushed pork rinds over the top.

8. Bake for about 25 minutes, until the dish is bubbling and the top is nicely browned, and serve.

NUTRITION:

Calories: 324; Fat: 11.5g; Protein: 5.1g; Carbohydrates: 2.2g.

AVOCADO CHIPS

PREPARATION TIME: 4 MINUTES | COOKING TIME: 8 MINUTES | SERVINGS: 2

INGREDIENTS:

1 de-seeded, peeled, sliced avocado

½ cup panko bread crumbs

¼ cup coconut flour

1 large beaten egg

1 teaspoon water

¼ teaspoon kosher salt

Cooking spray

DIRECTIONS:

1. First, preheat the air fryer to 400°F. Spray basket with cooking spray

2. Combine flour and salt in a container, egg and water in another, and panko bread crumbs in the last container. Dredge avocado slices in each, respectively.

3. Air fry for 4 minutes, flip the sides, and again fry until golden brown.

NUTRITION:

Calories: 320; Fat: 18g; Protein: 9.2g; Carbohydrates: 40g.

BAKED RADISHES

PREPARATION TIME: 10 MINUTES | COOKING TIME: 20 MINUTES | SERVINGS: 4

INGREDIENTS:

1 tablespoon chopped chives

15 sliced radishes

Salt

Vegetable oil cooking spray

Black pepper

DIRECTIONS:

1. Line your baking sheet well, then spray with the cooking spray.

2. Set the sliced radishes on the baking tray then sprinkle with cooking oil.

3. Add the seasonings then top with chives.

4. Set the oven for 10 minutes at 375°F, allow to bake.

5. Turn the radishes to bake for 10 minutes. Serve cold.

NUTRITION:

Calories: 63; Fat: 8g; Protein: 1g; Carbohydrates: 6g.

RELATIVELY FLAVORED GRATIN

PREPARATION TIME: 15 MINUTES | COOKING TIME: 46 MINUTES | SERVINGS: 8

INGREDIENTS:

½ cup heavy whipping cream

2 tablespoons butter

½ teaspoon garlic powder

¼ teaspoon xanthan gum

4 cups zucchini, sliced

1 small yellow onion, thinly sliced

Salt and freshly ground black pepper, to taste

1 ½ cups pepper jack cheese, shredded

DIRECTIONS:

1. Preheat the oven to 375°F and grease a 9×9-inch baking dish.

2. In a microwave-safe dish, place the heavy whipping cream, butter, garlic powder, and xanthan gum and microwave for about 1 minute.

3. Remove from microwave and beat the mixture until smooth.

4. Arrange 1/3 of zucchini and onion slices in the bottom of prepared baking dish and sprinkle with some salt, black pepper and cup pepper jack cheese.

5. Repeat the layers twice.

6. Now, place the cream mixture evenly on top.

7. Bake for about 45 minutes or until the top is golden brown.

8. Remove the baking dish from oven and set aside for about 5-10 minutes before serving.

9. Cut into 8 equal-sized portions and serve.

NUTRITION:

Calories: 140; Fat: 11.8g; Protein: 5.5g; Carbohydrates: 3.9g.

THANKSGIVING VEGGIE MEAL

PREPARATION TIME: 20 MINUTES | COOKING TIME: 30 MINUTES | SERVINGS: 6

INGREDIENTS:

For onion slices:

½ cup yellow onion, sliced very thinly

¼ cup almond flour

1/8 teaspoon garlic powder

Salt and freshly ground black pepper, to taste

For casserole:

1 pound fresh green beans, trimmed

1 tablespoon olive oil

8 ounces. fresh cremini mushrooms, sliced

½ cup yellow onion, thinly sliced

1/8 teaspoon garlic powder

Salt and freshly ground black pepper, to taste

1 teaspoon fresh thyme, chopped

½ cup homemade vegetable broth

½ cup sour cream

DIRECTIONS:

1. Preheat the oven to 350°F.
2. For onion slices: in a bowl, place all the ingredients and toss to coat well.
3. Arrange the onion slices onto a large baking sheet in a single layer.
4. In a pan of salted boiling water, add the green beans and cook for about 5 minutes.
5. Drain the green beans and transfer into a bowl of ice water.
6. Again, drain well and transfer into a large bowl.
7. In a large skillet, heat the oil over medium-high heat and sauté the mushrooms, onion, garlic powder, salt and black pepper for about 2-3 minutes.
8. Stir in the thyme, and broth and cook for about 3-5 minutes or until all the liquid is absorbed.
9. Remove from heat and transfer the mushroom mixture into the bowl with green beans.
10. Add the sour cream and stir to combine well.
11. Transfer the mixture into a 10-inch casserole dish.
12. Place the casserole dish and baking sheet of onion slices into the oven.
13. Bake for about 15-17 minutes.
14. Remove the baking dish from oven and let it cool for about 5 minutes before serving.
15. Top the casserole evenly with crispy onion slices.
16. Cut into 6 equal-sized portions and serve.

NUTRITION:

Calories: 134; Fat: 8.8g; Protein: 4.6g; Carbohydrates: 10g.

IDEAL COLD WEATHER STEW

COOKING TIME: 2 HOURS 40 MINUTES | PREPARATION TIME: 20 MINUTES | SERVINGS: 6

INGREDIENTS:

3 tablespoons olive oil, divided

8 ounces fresh mushrooms, quartered

1 ¼ pounds grass-fed beef chuck roast, trimmed and cubed into 1-inch size

2 tablespoons tomato paste

½ teaspoon dried thyme

1 bay leaf

5 cups homemade beef broth

6 ounces celery root, peeled and cubed

4 ounces yellow onions, chopped roughly

3 ounces carrot, peeled and sliced

2 garlic cloves, sliced

Salt and freshly ground black pepper, to taste

DIRECTIONS:

1. In a Dutch oven, heat 1 tablespoons of oil over medium heat and cook the mushrooms for about 2 minutes without stirring.

2. Stir the mushroom and cook for about 2 minutes more.

3. With a slotted spoon, transfer the mushroom onto a plate.

4. In the same pan, heat the remaining oil over medium-high heat and sear the beef cubes for about 4-5 minutes.

5. Stir in the tomato paste, thyme, and bay leaf and cook for about 1 minute.

6. Stir in the broth and bring to a boil.

7. Reduce the heat to low and simmer, covered for about 1½ hours.

8. Stir in the mushrooms, celery, onion, carrot, and garlic and simmers for about 40-60 minutes.

9. Stir in the salt and black pepper and remove from the heat.

10. Serve hot.

NUTRITION:

Calories: 447; Fat: 7.4g; Protein: 30.8g; Carbohydrates: 7.4g.

HUNGARIAN PORK STEW

COOKING TIME: 2 HOURS 20 MINUTES | PREPARATION TIME: 15 MINUTES | SERVINGS: 10

INGREDIENTS:

3 tablespoons olive oil

3 ½ pounds pork shoulder, cut into 4 portions

1 tablespoon butter

2 medium onions, chopped

16 ounces tomatoes, crushed

5 garlic cloves, crushed

2 Hungarian wax peppers, chopped

3 tablespoons Hungarian Sweet paprika

1 tablespoon smoked paprika

1 teaspoon hot paprika

½ teaspoon caraway seeds

1 bay leaf

1 cup homemade chicken broth

1 packet unflavored gelatin

2 tablespoons fresh lemon juice

Pinch of xanthan gum

Salt and freshly ground black pepper, to taste

DIRECTIONS:

1. In a heavy-bottomed pan, heat 1 tablespoon of oil over high heat and sear the pork for about 2-3 minutes or until browned.
2. Transfer the pork onto a plate and cut it into bite-sized pieces.
3. In the same pan, heat 1 tablespoon of oil and butter over medium-low heat and sauté the onions for about 5-6 minutes.
4. With a slotted spoon, transfer the onion into a bowl.
5. In the same pan, add the tomatoes and cook for about 3-4 minutes, without stirring.
6. Meanwhile, in a small frying pan, heat the remaining oil over low heat and sauté the garlic, wax peppers, all kinds of paprika, and caraway seeds for about 20-30 seconds.
7. Remove from the heat and set aside.
8. In a small bowl, mix together the gelatin and broth.
9. In the large pan, add the cooked pork, garlic mixture, gelatin mixture, and bay leaf and bring to a gentle boil.
10. Reduce the heat to low and simmer, covered for about 2 hours.
11. Stir in the xanthan gum and simmer for about 3-5 minutes.
12. Stir in the lemon juice, salt, and black pepper and remove from the heat.
13. Serve hot.

NUTRITION:

Calories: 529; Fat: 38.5g; Protein: 38.9g; Carbohydrates: 5.8g.

WILD MUSHROOM SOUP

PREPARATION TIME: 10 MINUTES | COOKING TIME: 30 MINUTES | SERVINGS: 4

INGREDIENTS:

6 ounces mix of portabella mushrooms, oyster mushrooms, and shiitake mushrooms

3 cups water

1 garlic clove

1 shallot

4 ounces butter

1 chicken bouillon cube

½ pound celery root

1 teaspoon thyme

1 tablespoon white wine vinegar

1 cup heavy whipping cream

Fresh parsley

DIRECTIONS:

1. Clean, trim, and chop your mushrooms and celery. Do the same to your shallot and garlic.
2. Sauté your chopped veggies in butter over medium heat in a saucepan.
3. Add thyme, vinegar, chicken bouillon cube, and water as you bring to boil. Then let it simmer for 10-15 minutes.
4. Add cream to them with an immersion blender until your desired consistency. Serve with parsley on top.

NUTRITION:

Calories: 481; Fat: 47g; Protein: 7g; Carbohydrates: 9g.

ZUCCHINI CREAM SOUP

PREPARATION TIME: 5 MINUTES | COOKING TIME: 20 MINUTES | SERVINGS: 4

INGREDIENTS:

3 zucchinis

32 ounces chicken broth

2 cloves garlic

2 tablespoons sour cream

½ small onion

Parmesan cheese (for topping if desired)

DIRECTIONS:

1. Combine your broth, garlic, zucchini, and onion in a large pot over medium heat until boiling.

2. Lower the heat, cover, and let simmer for 15-20 minutes.

3. Remove from heat and purée with an immersion blender, while adding the sour cream and pureeing until smooth.

4. Season to taste and top with your cheese.

NUTRITION:

Calories: 117; Fat: 9g; Protein: 4g; Carbohydrates: 3g.

CAULIFLOWER SOUP

PREPARATION TIME: 5 MINUTES | COOKING TIME: 25 MINUTES | SERVINGS: 6

INGREDIENTS:

32 ounces vegetable broth

1 head cauliflower, diced

2 garlic cloves, minced

1 onion, diced

½ tablespoon olive oil

Salt and pepper

Grated Parmesan, sliced green onion for topping

DIRECTIONS:

1. In a pot, heat oil over medium heat, while adding the onion and garlic. Then cook them for 4-5 minutes.

2. Add in the cauliflower and vegetable broth. Boil it and then cover for 15-20 minutes while covered.

3. Pour all contents of pot into a blender and season it.

4. Blend until smooth. Top it with your cheese and green onion.

NUTRITION:

Calories: 37; Fat: 1g; Protein: 3g; Carbohydrates: 3g.

THAI COCONUT SOUP

PREPARATION TIME: 10 MINUTES | COOKING TIME: 35 MINUTES | SERVINGS: 4

INGREDIENTS:

3 chicken breasts

9 ounces coconut milk

9 ounces chicken broth

2/3 tablespoon chili sauce

18 ounces water

2/3 tablespoon coconut aminos

2/3 ounce lime juice

2/3 teaspoon ground ginger

¼ cup red boat fish sauce

Salt and pepper

DIRECTIONS:

1. Slice up the chicken breasts thinly. Make them bite-sized.

2. In a large stock pot, mix your coconut milk, water, fish sauce, chili sauce, lime juice, ginger, coconut aminos, and broth. Bring to a boil.

3. Stir in chicken pieces. Then reduce the heat and cover pot, while simmering for 30 minutes.

4. Season them and enjoy.

NUTRITION:

Calories: 227; Fat: 17g; Protein: 19g; Carbohydrates: 3g.

CHICKEN RAMEN SOUP

PREPARATION TIME: 10 MINUTES | COOKING TIME: 20 MINUTES | SERVINGS: 2

INGREDIENTS:

1 chicken breast

2 eggs

1 zucchini, made into noodles

4 cups chicken broth

2 cloves garlic, peeled and minced

2 tablespoons coconut aminos

3 tablespoons avocado oil

1 tablespoon ginger

DIRECTIONS:

1. Pan-fry the chicken in avocado oil in a pan until brown.

2. Hard boil your eggs and slice them in half.

3. Add chicken broth to a large pot and simmer with the garlic, coconut aminos, and ginger. Then add in the zucchini noodles for 4-5 minutes.

4. Put the broth into a bowl, top it with eggs and chicken slices, and season to your liking.

NUTRITION:

Calories: 478; Fat: 39g; Protein: 31g; Carbohydrates: 3g.

CREAMY MIXED SEAFOOD SOUP

PREPARATION TIME: 15 MINUTES | COOKING TIME: 15 MINUTES | SERVINGS: 4

INGREDIENTS:

1 tablespoon avocado oil

2 garlic cloves, minced

¾ tablespoon almond flour

1 cup vegetable broth

1 teaspoon dried dill

1 pound frozen mixed seafood

Salt and black pepper to taste

1 tablespoon plain vinegar

2 cups cooking cream

Fresh dill leaves to garnish

DIRECTIONS:

1. Heat oil, sauté the garlic for 30 seconds or until fragrant.

2. Stir in the almond flour until brown.

3. Mix in the vegetable broth until smooth and stir in the dill, seafood mix, salt, and black pepper.

4. Bring the soup to a boil and then simmer for 3 to 4 minutes or until the seafood cooks.

5. Add the vinegar, cooking cream, and stir well. Garnish with dill, serve.

NUTRITION:

Calories: 361; Fat: 12.4g; Protein: 11.7g; Carbohydrates: 3.9g.

DESSERT RECIPES

COCONUT PUDDING

PREPARATION TIME: 15 MINUTES | COOKING TIME: 5 MINUTES | SERVINGS: 4

INGREDIENTS:

1 ½ cups unsweetened almond milk, divided

1 tablespoon unflavored powdered gelatin

1 cup unsweetened coconut milk

1/3 cup Swerve

3 tablespoons cacao powder

2 teaspoons instant coffee granules

6 drops liquid stevia

DIRECTIONS:

1. In a large bowl, add 1/2 cup of almond milk and sprinkle evenly with gelatin.
2. Set aside until soaked.
3. In a pan, add the remaining almond milk, coconut milk, Swerve, cacao powder, coffee granules, and stevia and bring to a gentle boil, stirring continuously.
4. Remove from the heat.
5. In a blender, add the gelatin mixture, and hot milk mixture and pulse until smooth.
6. Transfer the mixture into serving glasses and set aside to cool completely.
7. With plastic wrap, cover each glass and refrigerate for about 3-4 hours before serving.

NUTRITION:

Calories: 136; Fat: 12.1g; Protein: 4.4g; Carbohydrates: 5.8g.

PRETTY BLUEBERRY BITES

PREPARATION TIME: 20 MINUTES | COOKING TIME: 0 MINUTES | SERVINGS: 10

INGREDIENTS:

1 scoop unsweetened whey Protein powder

½ cup coconut flour, sifted

1-2 tablespoon granulated Erythritol

¼ teaspoon ground cinnamon

Pinch of salt

¼ cup dried unsweetened blueberries

½-1 cup unsweetened almond milk

DIRECTIONS:

1. Line a large baking sheet with parchment paper. Set aside.
2. In a large bowl, add the protein powder, flour, Erythritol, cinnamon, and salt and mix well.
3. Add the blueberries and stir to combine.
4. Gradually, add the desired amount of the almond milk and mix until a dough is formed.
5. Immediately, make desired sized balls from the blueberry mixture.
6. Arrange the balls onto the prepared baking sheet in a single layer.
7. Refrigerate to set for about 30 minutes before serving.

NUTRITION:

Calories: 18; Fat: 0.4g; Protein: 2.4g; Carbohydrates: 1.3g.

COLD MINI MUFFINS

PREPARATION TIME: 20 MINUTES | COOKING TIME: 2 MINUTES | SERVINGS: 24

INGREDIENTS:

20 ounces 70% dark chocolate chips, divided

¼ cup coconut butter, softened

24 whole almonds

DIRECTIONS:

1. Line 24 cups of a mini muffin tin with paper liners. Set aside.

2. In a microwave-safe bowl, add 3/4 of chocolate chips and microwave on High for about 1 minute, stirring once halfway through.

3. Remove from microwave and stir well.

4. Divide the melted chocolate into prepared muffin cups evenly and refrigerate until set completely.

5. In a microwave-safe bowl, add the remaining chocolate chips and microwave on High for about 1 minute, stirring once halfway through.

6. Remove from microwave and stir well.

7. Remove from the refrigerator and t top each chocolate cup with the softened coconut butter evenly, followed by the remaining melted chocolate.

8. Gently, insert 1 almond in each cup and refrigerate until set before serving.

NUTRITION:

Calories: 151; Fat: 14.7g; Protein: 3.6g; Carbohydrates: 7.1g.

CHOCOLATE LOVER'S MUFFINS

PREPARATION TIME: 15 MINUTES | COOKING TIME: 20 MINUTES | SERVINGS: 6

INGREDIENTS:

4 tablespoons almond flour

2 tablespoons coconut flour

2 tablespoons beet powder

1 tablespoon organic baking powder

2 organic eggs

1 teaspoon liquid stevia

3 tablespoons unsweetened almond milk

1/2 teaspoon organic vanilla extract

1/3 cup 70% dark chocolate

DIRECTIONS:

1. Preheat the oven to 375°F. Grease 6 cups of a muffin tin.
2. In a bowl, add the flours, beet powder and baking powder and mix well.
3. In another large bowl, add the eggs, stevia, almond milk and vanilla extract and beat until well-combined.
4. Add the flour mixture and mix until just combined.
5. Gently, fold in the chocolate chips.
6. Place the mixture into the prepared muffin cups evenly.
7. Bake for about 15-20 minutes or until a toothpick inserted in the center comes out clean.
8. Remove from the oven and place the muffin tin onto a wire rack to cool for about 10 minutes.
9. Carefully invert the muffins onto the wire rack to cool completely before serving.

NUTRITION:

Calories: 152; Fat: 9.9g; Protein: 5.2g; Carbohydrates: 10.2g.

COCOA BROWNIES

PREPARATION TIME: 10 MINUTES | COOKING TIME: 30 MINUTES | SERVINGS: 9 SERVINGS

INGREDIENTS:

½ cup salted butter, melted

1 cup Granular Swerve Sweetener

2 large eggs

2 teaspoons vanilla extract

12 squares unsweetened baking chocolate, melted

2 tablespoons coconut flour

2 tablespoons cocoa powder

½ teaspoon baking powder

½ teaspoon salt

½ cup walnuts, chopped (optional)

DIRECTIONS:

1. Preheat oven to 350°F.
2. Spray square baking pan with cooking spray or grease pan well with butter.
3. In a large mixing bowl, use an electric mixer or whisk and mix together butter and sweetener.
4. Add the eggs and vanilla extract to bowl and mix with an electric mixer for 1 minute until smooth.
5. Add melted chocolate and stir with a wooden spoon or spatula until the chocolate is incorporated into the butter mixture.
6. In a separate bowl, mix the dry ingredients (remaining ingredients besides walnuts) until combined.
7. Add dry ingredients into the bowl with the wet ingredients and stir with a wooden spoon until combined.
8. Add walnuts if desired.
9. Pour batter into prepared pan. Spread to cover the entire bottom of the pan and into corners.
10. Place in the center rack of the oven and bake for 30 minutes.
11. After the brownies are baked, take them out and leave them in the pan to cool.
12. When cool, cut them into 9 servings, and they are ready to eat.
13. These have to be as a once-in-a-while treat because they are sweet, and if you're like me, that sugar will continue to call your name. These are so good you will have to work to eat only one serving.

NUTRITION:

Calories: 201; Fat: 19g; Protein: 3g; Carbohydrates: 5g.

CHOCOLATE CHIP COOKIES

PREPARATION TIME: 10 MINUTES | COOKING TIME: 20 MINUTES | SERVINGS: 24 COOKIES

INGREDIENTS:

1 ½ cups almond flour

1 teaspoon baking powder

½ teaspoon salt

½ cup butter, softened

½ cup stevia

1 teaspoon vanilla extract

1 large egg

1 cup sugar-free chocolate chips

½ cup nuts, chopped

DIRECTIONS:

1. Preheat oven to 350°F.

2. Grease cookie sheets with butter and set aside.

3. In a large bowl, cream together the butter and the stevia.

4. Add the large egg and vanilla extract to the butter and stevia.

5. Mix until the egg is incorporated into the butter.

6. In a second bowl, mix together almond flour, baking powder, and salt until mixed well.

7. Add dry ingredients to the large bowl and mix until it is combined.

8. Add sugar-free chocolate chips and nuts and stir until they are distributed evenly.

9. Drop by spoonfuls onto the cookie sheet.

10. Bake until golden brown and the surface of cookies appear dry on the top and are cooked all the way through.

11. Remove cookies from sheet to a wire rack to cool.

12. Make these with or without nuts. Cocoa nibs can be used in place of the sugar-free chocolate chips. This is a good recipe to keep on hand, so you can have a cookie along with everyone else. Make it a fun project with kids or friends. Baking is always a good way to bring people together, and this is a recipe everyone will enjoy.

NUTRITION:

Calories: 120; Fat: 11g; Protein: 2g; Carbohydrates: 3g.

KETO BROWN BUTTER PRALINES

PREPARATION TIME: 6 MINUTES | COOKING TIME: 10 MINUTES | SERVINGS: 10 SERVINGS

INGREDIENTS:

2 sticks salted butter

⅔cup heavy cream

⅔cup monk fruit sweetener

½ teaspoon xanthan gum

2 cups pecans, chopped

Sea salt

DIRECTIONS:

1. Prepare a cookie sheet with parchment paper or a silicone baking mat.

2. In a medium-size, medium weight saucepan, brown the butter until it smells nutty. Don't burn the butter. This will take about 5 minutes.

3. Stir in heavy cream, xanthan gum, and sweetener.

4. Take the pan off the heat and stir in the nuts.

5. Place pan in the refrigerator for an hour.

6. Stir the mixture occasionally while it is getting colder.

7. After an hour, scoop the mixture onto the cookie sheets and shape into cookies.

8. Sprinkle with sea salt.

9. Refrigerate on the cookies sheet until the pralines are hard.

10. After the cookies are hard, transfer to an airtight container in the refrigerator.

11. This is a special treat. A low carb praline with the fat from the butter and creamis a nice dessert to have on a special occasion that you can work into your day without totally messing up your macros. The monk fruit sweetener is a 1:1 measure, so the texture is not altered by not using sugar. Give them a try, and you will not be disappointed.

NUTRITION:

Calories: 338; Fat: 36g; Protein: 2g; Carbohydrates: 1g.

RASPBERRY PUDDING SURPRISE

PREPARATION TIME: 20 MINUTES | COOKING TIME: 20 MINUTES | SERVINGS: 1 SERVING

INGREDIENTS:

3 tablespoons chia seeds

½ cup unsweetened almond milk

1 scoop chocolate protein powder

¼ cup raspberries, fresh or frozen

1 teaspoon honey

DIRECTIONS:

1. Combine the almond milk, protein powder and chia seeds together.

2. Let rest for 5 minutes before stirring.

3. Refrigerate for 30 minutes.

4. Top with raspberries. Serve!

NUTRITION:

Calories: 225; Fat: 21g; Protein: 3g; Carbohydrates: 3g.

WHITE CHOCOLATE BERRY CHEESECAKE

PREPARATION TIME: 10 MINUTES | COOKING TIME: 0 MINUTES | SERVINGS: 4 SERVINGS

INGREDIENTS:

8 ounces cream cheese, softened

2 ounces heavy cream

½ teaspoon Splenda

1 teaspoon raspberries

1 tablespoon Da Vinci Sugar-Free syrup, white chocolate flavor

DIRECTIONS:

1. Whip together the ingredients to a thick consistency.

2. Divide into cups.

3. Refrigerate.

4. Serve!

NUTRITION:

Calories: 330; Fat: 29g; Protein: 6g; Carbohydrates: 6g.

CURRY POWDER

PREPARATION TIME: 10 MINUTES | COOKING TIME: 10 MINUTES | SERVINGS: 20

INGREDIENTS:

¼ cup coriander seeds

2 tablespoons mustard seeds

2 tablespoons cumin seeds

2 tablespoons anise seeds

1 tablespoon whole allspice berries

1 tablespoon fenugreek seeds

5 tablespoons ground turmeric

DIRECTIONS:

1. In a large nonstick frying pan, place all the spices except turmeric over medium heat and cook for about 9-10 minutes or until toasted completely, stirring continuously.

2. Remove the frying pan from heat and set aside to cool.

3. In a spice grinder, add the toasted spices and turmeric, and grind until a fine powder forms.

4. Transfer into an airtight jar to preserve.

NUTRITION:

Calories: 18; Fat: 0.8g; Protein: 0.8g; Carbohydrates: 2.7g.

POULTRY SEASONING

PREPARATION TIME: 5 MINUTES | COOKING TIME: 0 MINUTES | SERVINGS: 10

INGREDIENTS:

2 teaspoons dried sage, crushed finely

1 teaspoon dried marjoram, crushed finely

¾ teaspoon dried rosemary, crushed finely

1 ½ teaspoons dried thyme, crushed finely

½ teaspoon ground nutmeg

½ teaspoon ground black pepper

DIRECTIONS:

1. Add all the ingredients to a bowl and stir to combine.

2. Transfer into an airtight jar to preserve.

NUTRITION:

Calories: 2; Fat: 0.1g; Protein: 0.1g; Carbohydrates: 0.4g.

BASIL PESTO

PREPARATION TIME: 10 MINUTES | COOKING TIME: 0 MINUTES | SERVINGS: 6

INGREDIENTS:

2 cups fresh basil

4 garlic cloves, peeled

2/3 cup Parmesan cheese, grated

1/3 cup pine nuts

½ cup olive oil

Salt and ground black pepper, as required

DIRECTIONS:

1. Place the basil, garlic, Parmesan cheese, and pine nuts in a food processor, and pulse until a chunky mixture is formed.

2. While the motor is running gradually, add the oil and pulse until smooth.

3. Now, add the salt and black pepper, and pulse until well combined.

4. Serve immediately.

NUTRITION:

Calories: 232; Fat: 24.2g; Protein: 5g; Carbohydrates: 1.9g.

BBQ SAUCE

PREPARATION TIME: 15 MINUTES | COOKING TIME: 20 MINUTES | SERVINGS: 20

INGREDIENTS:

2 ½ (6-ounce) cans sugar-free tomato paste

½ cup organic apple cider vinegar

1/3 cup powdered erythritol

2 tablespoons Worcestershire sauce

1 tablespoon liquid smoke

2 teaspoons smoked paprika

1 teaspoon garlic powder

½ teaspoon onion powder

Salt, as required

¼ teaspoon red chili powder

¼ teaspoon cayenne pepper

1 ½ cups water

DIRECTIONS:

1. Add all the ingredients (except the water) to a pan and beat until well combined.

2. Add 1 cup of water and beat until combined.

3. Add the remaining water and beat until well combined.

4. Place the pan over medium-high heat and bring to a gentle boil.

5. Adjust the heat to medium-low and simmer, uncovered for about 20 minutes, stirring frequently.

6. Remove the pan of sauce from the heat and set aside to cool slightly before serving.

7. You can preserve this sauce in the refrigerator by placing it into an airtight container.

NUTRITION:

Calories: 22; Fat: 0.1g; Protein: 1g; Carbohydrates: 4.7g.

KETCHUP

PREPARATION TIME: 10 MINUTES | COOKING TIME: 30 MINUTES | SERVINGS: 12

INGREDIENTS:

6 ounces sugar-free tomato paste

1 cup water

¼ cup powdered erythritol

3 tablespoons balsamic vinegar

½ teaspoon garlic powder

½ teaspoon onion powder

¼ teaspoon paprika

1/8 teaspoon ground cloves

1/8 teaspoon mustard powder

Salt, as required

DIRECTIONS:

1. Add all ingredients to a small pan and beat until smooth.
2. Now, place the pan over medium heat and bring to a gentle simmer, stirring continuously.
3. Adjust the heat to low and simmer, covered for about 30 minutes or until desired thickness, stirring occasionally.
4. Remove the pan from heat and with an immersion blender, blend until smooth.
5. Now, set aside to cool completely before serving.
6. You can preserve this ketchup in the refrigerator by placing it in an airtight container.

NUTRITION:

Calories: 13; Fat: 0.1g; Protein: 0.7g; Carbohydrates: 2.9g.

CRANBERRY SAUCE

PREPARATION TIME: 10 MINUTES | COOKING TIME: 15 MINUTES | SERVINGS: 6

INGREDIENTS:

12 ounces fresh cranberries

1 cup powdered erythritol

¾ cup water

1 teaspoon fresh lemon zest, grated

½ teaspoon organic vanilla extract

DIRECTIONS:

1. Place the cranberries, water, erythritol, and lemon zest in a medium pan and mix well.
2. Place the pan over medium heat and bring to a boil.
3. Adjust the heat to low and simmer for about 12-15 minutes, stirring frequently.
4. Remove the pan from heat and mix in the vanilla extract.
5. Set aside at room temperature to cool completely.
6. Transfer the sauce into a bowl and refrigerate to chill before serving.

NUTRITION:

Calories: 32; Fat: 0.2g; Protein: 0g; Carbohydrates: 5.3g.

YOGURT TZATZIKI

PREPARATION TIME: 10 MINUTES | COOKING TIME: 0 MINUTES | SERVINGS: 12

INGREDIENTS:

1 large English cucumber, peeled and grated

Salt, as required

2 cups plain Greek yogurt

1 tablespoon fresh lemon juice

4 garlic cloves, minced

1 tablespoon fresh mint leaves, chopped

2 tablespoons fresh dill, chopped

Pinch of cayenne pepper

Ground black pepper, as required

DIRECTIONS:

1. Arrange a colander in the sink.
2. Place the cucumber into the colander and sprinkle with salt.
3. Let it drain for about 10-15 minutes.
4. With your hands, squeeze the cucumber well.
5. Place the cucumber and remaining ingredients in a large bowl and stir to combine.
6. Cover the bowl and place in the refrigerator to chill for at least 4-8 hours before serving.

NUTRITION:

Calories: 36; Fat: 0.6g; Protein: 2.7g; Carbohydrates: 4.5g.

ALMOND BUTTER

PREPARATION TIME: 10 MINUTES | COOKING TIME: 15 MINUTES | SERVINGS: 8

INGREDIENTS:

2 ¼ cups raw almonds

1 tablespoon coconut oil

¾ teaspoon salt

4-6 drops liquid stevia

½ teaspoon ground cinnamon

DIRECTIONS:

1. Preheat your oven to 325°F.
2. Arrange the almonds onto a rimmed baking sheet in an even layer.
3. Bake for about 12-15 minutes.
4. Remove the almonds from the oven and let them cool completely.
5. In a food processor, fitted with a metal blade, place the almonds and pulse until a fine meal forms.
6. Add the coconut oil and salt, and pulse for about 6-9 minutes.
7. Add the stevia and cinnamon, and pulse for about 1-2 minutes.
8. You can preserve this almond butter in the refrigerator by placing it into an airtight container.

NUTRITION:

Calories: 170; Fat: 15.1; Protein: 5.7g; Carbohydrates: 5.8g.

LEMON CURD SPREAD

PREPARATION TIME: 10 MINUTES | COOKING TIME: 10 MINUTES | SERVINGS: 20

INGREDIENTS:

3 large organic eggs

½ cup powdered erythritol

¼ cup fresh lemon juice

2 teaspoons lemon zest, grated

4 tablespoons butter, cut into 3 pieces

DIRECTIONS:

1. In a glass bowl, place the eggs, erythritol, lemon juice, and lemon zest.

2. Arrange the glass bowl over a pan of barely simmering water and soak for about 10 minutes or until the mixture becomes thick, beating continuously.

3. Remove from heat and immediately stir in the butter.

4. Set aside for about 2-3 minutes.

5. With a wire whisk, beat until smooth and creamy.

NUTRITION:

Calories: 32; Fat: 3.1; Protein: 1g; Carbohydrates: 0.2g.

TAHINI SPREAD

PREPARATION TIME: 10 MINUTES | COOKING TIME: 0 MINUTES | SERVINGS: 4

INGREDIENTS:

¼ cup tahini

2 garlic cloves, peeled

3 tablespoons olive oil

3 tablespoons water

1 ½ tablespoons fresh lemon juice

¼ teaspoon ground cumin

Salt and ground black pepper, as required

DIRECTIONS:

1. Place all of the ingredients in a high-speed blender and pulse until creamy.

2. Pour the smoothie into two glasses and serve immediately.

NUTRITION:

Calories: 183; Fat: 18.7; Protein: 2.7g; Carbohydrates: 3.9g.

MEASUREMENT AND CONVERSIONS

CUPS	OZ	G	TBSP	TSP	ML
1	8	225	16	48	250
3/4	6	170	12	36	175
2/3	5	140	11	32	150
1/2	4	115	8	24	125
1/3	3	70	5	16	70
1/4	2	60	4	12	60
1/8	1	30	2	6	30
1/16	1/2	15	1	3	15

250°F	300°F	325°F	350°F	400°F	450°F
120°C	150°F	160°C	175°C	200°C	230°C

Printed in Great Britain
by Amazon

74442427R00122